The Girl Collection

The Girl Collection

A Novel

R.M. Cobetto

ISBN 979-8-218-67498-4 (ebook)
ISBN 979-8-218-67500-4 (paperback)
ISBN 979-8-218-67501-1 (hardback)

Dedication

To K. I love you so desperately. Thank you for forcing my hand to write.

Acknowledgements

Thank you to Gabe McCarthy for being the best friend I could ask for and supporting this project wholeheartedly. Many thanks to Kieran Devaney for your thoughtful edits and your openness to spontaneous change throughout the process. To Roderick Brydon, thank you for designing a beautiful cover that captures the spirit of the story. Thank you to members of the New Orleans Write or Die group for your eyes and your unwavering support. In the same vein, thank you to Third Lantern Lit and all that you offer to local writers. To She Wants Revenge, thank you for making the soundtrack to which I wrote this!

Part 1

Why She Did It

Her eyes opened into the din of fluorescence. *Was any of that real?* This was the psychiatric floor of the University Medical Center, where RollsUponPrank was freshly admitted for spitting in a policeman's face. Her parents and landlord had already been contacted; all assured the doctors that petty assault was out of character for the young woman. The authorities were quickly convinced this was an isolated episode, likely drug-induced. They pressed no charges against her.

But RollsUponPrank found no comfort in their lenience. She was now alive to a disturbing truth, and her heart was rattling, discordant, with oppressive love. The techs and nurses had all pitched up their brows at the rate of her pulse. She turned toward the smooth pine shelving unit, bolted to the wall, and gazed along the spines of her lover's books—wondering how he'd gotten them inside.

She wondered if anything that happened in the last week would stay real, or if it would all die like low fog in slow warmth. It seemed delusional to think that a phone could drive her insane; she must have been insane already—or just half-insane, which she already knew herself to be. The doctors remained undecided.

Though the ones she met had joined in a chorus of validation. She explained her predicament: when a certain type of man decides he likes you, he hacks your phone. And if he decides he wants to make you suffer, he lets it record and stream your daily life, half as porn and half as comedy.

Not only did the doctors agree that this happens, but they were so amused to meet one of these girls—a live one—who had caught on, even bit back. They hardly knew how to speak to her. Most retreated into jargon or innuendo.

Being a unit of intensive observation, even the bathrooms were equipped with hidden cameras. When RollsUponPrank emerged from her morning shower, with her hair neatly braided into two wet plaits that hung down to her nipples, one of the doctors squicked down the yellowed linoleum hall to see her straight away. "How was your shower," he asked, "was the water pressure okay? Sometimes it isn't as strong as I would like." He was delighted that she understood the implication and that she banked it as neutral.

RollsUponPrank had spit in that cop's face—with some enjoyment—not because she was angry with him for simply being a man, and not because he had personally violated her in any way. She had done it because he tried to tell her what to do in a context where she calculated that he had no right.

That right belonged to Meta_king—her hacker—and it belonged to him alone.

Modeling

When RollsUponPrank made her debut as a webcam model, she was only nineteen years old. These were the early days of independent online porn, when it was a chitinous digital tundra, hardcore and sparsely populated. Girls danced in undulating loops on a mosaic screen of expectant parts, or they simply lounged on their beds and waited for remote visitors.

She worked on a site that sorted the grid of girls by standard metrics: age; popularity; age of account; body measurements; hair color; nationality; skills; et cetera. When she debuted, her image soon floated to the very top of the gallery, gazing out from behind a latex mask. It looked half gothic and half cartoonish, in a lucha libre sort of way.

The girl fancied herself a student of men. And of course, she wanted a band or two from the pile of unclaimed cash she knew to be buried there. She also liked the opportunity to spin any yarn she liked, with an ethical audience.

RollsUponPrank felt a bit fey in her dealings with men—real, living men with bodies—so she particularly enjoyed the freedom that distance granted her. It served up the excitement of love within the slippery comfort of the surreal. I am sure most readers will find something sympathetic in her yearning.

Each morning, as she affixed a painty red lacquer to her lips and dabbed an orange blossom cologne to the skin she freshly shaved, she wondered what the men would ask for that day, with only her disembodied eyes to judge them.

She would put on a slow, sensual record and practice moving to the rhythm in an easy, inviting way for her public stream. This was surprisingly boring to do at length—downright intolerable for more than half an hour—so it was a great relief when some patron entered her chat room. At least then she could tell a story. It was a greater relief still when someone requested a private session, where she could act one out. Even on the short, non-narrative calls, she still preferred to simulate sex than entice with repetitive dance.

RollsUponPrank was not afraid to be seen as or treated like a whore, however meager that distinction may be, and however cruel it may sound. As long as she could fashion it a performance and herself a character, the feeling couldn't cling to her so tight. She saw it as an endurance exercise.

She had protected herself as a highly sexual young girl behind a shield of chubbiness and poor hygiene—and while it had worked, at times, to avert her father's eyes, the strategy chafed at her self image. Modeling was part of her quest to feel loved within the soft confines of pretending. It was her life's work.

And so, in her desire, RollsUponPrank entered the game with no concern for—or awareness of—the security risks. She hadn't entertained that line of thought, that she could be exposed in a way she didn't want.

In a more general sense, she always preferred to deal with tangible matters over conceptual ones. Could you rub, imbibe, inhale it? Then she was interested. You might call RollsUponPrank a material girl.

Meta_king

RollsUponPrank went to college with Meta_king, but the two had never spoken—not even once. They had gone to a specialized college for teenagers who skipped several years of high school—so they shared a common condition, socially— and the campus was so small and isolated that, by all rights, they should have gotten closer than they had.

RollsUponPrank had a brooding but naive aura that gripped Meta_king's boyish imagination. She also had a spooky pallor and wiry copper coils of hair that carried his curious mind to the Aran islands, which then made him imagine the video game girls he loved who battled space pirates and dressed like cavewomen of the future.

Not only was Meta_king too busy—even at that typically unserious age of sixteen—to follow every fleeting crush he felt, but he had also heard the rumors about the girl and knew to keep his distance. He knew that she had a deeply troubled mind, she told all kinds of wild lies, and she could fly into a humiliating rage (for all parties) or an equally stultifying depression for almost any reason.

RollsUponPrank, too, had noticed Meta_king. In her eyes, he stood out as the most impressive specimen on the caravan of geeks. While most of her peers knew Meta_king as a physics prodigy who sparkled in all the school's promotional brochures, wearing starched shirts and a starched (but genuine) smile, RollsUponPrank admired him as a dancer. She noticed the ropes of muscle twisting lines from his wrists down to his groin, and also noticed the way he carefully covered them in button-down shirts, refusing to lead with his—in her eyes—powerful physicality.

RollsUponPrank supposed that she liked Meta_king, but she had placed him out of reach to protect her comically tortured heart. The rumors were true; she was implacable and raw, the sort of girl who would skip parties to cry in the bathtub, but still played 'please, mister' outside of the liquor store. She had emerged from puberty as the sort of animal who attracts mean older men. She had already begun to embrace that lot in life, even at her would-be-tender age.

So the first time that RollsUponPrank spoke to Meta_king, he was anonymous and she was naked except for the black latex mask. Still, his voice roused a strange feeling inside of her overprotected heart. It was so resonant, as if he was used to making bold statements and watching them take substance in front of him, like a wizard or a chemist. It brought an awareness of reality to her little sexual sandbox, where she was so used to making up stories and even lying flatly about the most basic facts of her life.

Of course she knew, on some core level, that it was imperative in her work to keep the defenses airtight. But she simply couldn't picture Meta_king's voice, hard and clear and sweet, causing her any harm at all. Even detached from his body, face, and name, as it was in their call.

On the other end, Meta_king was amazed to see RollsUponPrank naked in front of him and willing to do whatever he might ask, when before he had known her as a chaotic—and often destructive—force who never noticed boys her own age. He was thrilled to be the first to catch her.

He felt it from his first utterance on their call—her eyes registered knowledge. She knew his voice even though she didn't realize it.

Magical Ailment

RollsUponPrank didn't know it, but she was bipolar. If you're fanciful, this could mean she had something like a fairy godmother, part of her who lived in a chamber of ill-gotten finery, who slept light in the shadow of anything, and who always had a rough-hewn, monumental fix for all her problems. RollsUponPrank saw it that way.

Like many others with her affliction, she trusted the magic and dodged any pressure to tamp it down. This part of her psyche was suited to handle danger, and it charged her life with excitement. In her view, they had a wonderful relationship.

Class Together

RollsUponPrank and Meta_king had taken just one class together at their special school. *Game Theory.* She gazed lazily over the shoulders of her peers—aslant from hours playing video games and reading crooked—and looked straight into the back of Meta_king's head. Her own posture was far too stiff for a girl her age, always braced for a hungry touch from out of sight.

She was just trying to satisfy a course requirement—it was a liberal arts school, after all, and she was expected to graduate with a general smattering of knowledge that would leave any type of company feeling slightly edified and far more enchanting than they would with an untrained ear. So she sat in this economics course full of boys with greater acumen than her own in math and science—but not in human behavior.

She found it overwrought, how they tried to calculate rewards and negative incentives, when she had always made such judgments in the moment or left them up to chance.

Many of the problems cast a boy against a girl for the syntactical ease of opposite pronouns. *Maybe that's why boys can be so mean,* she thought. *They were trying to protect their own payout before some girl could do the same. But why would you think of love as a prisoners' dilemma?* She chewed the cap of an alien green pen. It made no sense to her.

Social Engineering

Shortly after RollsUponPrank made her debut in indie online porn, Meta_king sent an anonymous request for an hour and a half of her time. This was a curiously long assignation with a price tag of six hundred dollars. This number, and the speed with which it might appear, was enough to truly titillate her—she could pay her rent for a month in those days, or maybe buy another latex outfit to embody a different character.

She went to work preparing for the show. She slicked her body down with a pat of coconut oil, which made her chalky skin glow brighter and added a layer of visual interest for the camera. Then she went to gather and clean an assortment of colorful toys cast in metal and glass and silicone. She frothed a sulfur yellow bar of soap and massaged the bubbles over their inventive shapes, plotting which ones she'd actually use, and in what sequence.

Then she picked on a pair of ripped fishnets, studiously swiped her lips with a doefoot applicator, and pressed "record".

Meta_king had been waiting in—carefully contained—boyish delight on the other end, shown as a grey square on her screen. Immediately when her body appeared, shining and crawling across the floor toward the computer, he surprised her with a question. "If you were my pet," he asked aloud from his private space, "what kind of animal would you be?"

RollsUponPrank was disarmed by the mixture of bravado and wholesomeness. She considered her pet-self, and whether she had one—she had been told before that she moved like a feline, in her uncanny flexibility and strange postures, so the couple jointly determined that she would be a black cat.

Meta_king encouraged her to slide around on the wooden floors and display her body in various feline angles and poses. He asked her to contort herself, to lick the back of her thigh, and to meow for him—all of this, and his voice showed no indication of arousal. Only a detached amusement.

RollsUponPrank had an exaggerated sheen now from the sweat and the oil, which was mixing into a plasticky perfume in the heat of the lights behind her computer. As the first hour passed, Meta_king gently coaxed her into more degrading, or perhaps more realistic, acts. The distinction is, of course, a personal one.

But she didn't find it degrading to be an animal, and especially not such a clean and graceful one as a cat. So she obliged each of Meta_king's requests with a genuine desire to satisfy him.

She couldn't pinpoint what his deeper desire was, beyond the high of domination. In her girlish mind she figured that there must be some conflicting impulse behind his requests—another anchor point to create an exciting inner tension. Why else would he stage this if he wasn't aroused?

She felt a twinge in her gut that signified nothing to her mind. Perhaps it was fear, apprehension, or concern. It was overpowered by her sense of ease within this royal voice.

When she reached for her water bottle, Meta_king's voice cut her off. "Cats don't use their hands to drink," he said. "What do cats do?"

"They use their tongue?" RollsUponPrank knew the answer, but she also knew to phrase it as a question.

"That's right," Meta_king said, "they use their tongue."

So RollsUponPrank twisted the bottle open and spilled some water over her sternum. It dripped down between her breasts, to the inward curves of her stomach, over her lower belly, down to her slightly parted thighs. The water finally pooled on the floor around her knees. "Drink it," Meta_king commanded.

RollsUponPrank drank it. She positioned herself at a flattering angle for the computer, and she bent down to taste the pool of oily water. Then she licked the floor slowly and carefully until it shone only with her own saliva.

"Good kitty," Meta_king said. And then she heard his rocky laugh as he said her full legal name. "Goodbye." And the call ended, with none of the usual fanfare.

This sent a shiver through her body as she knelt there on the floor, still wearing her mask and fishnets. How did he know her name, and what happened to the money? How had she let this voice charm her into neglecting the very first rule: collect the payment first?

Shaken and confused, she fired off an email in a pointless attempt to extract an answer. But Meta_king would not respond to her; not for many, many years.

To: sdtr304z9@gmail.com
From: ecandy1993@gmail.com
Subject: What happened?

I'm not even concerned about the money at this point. All I want to know is, why did you lie? I don't understand.

Pap Smear

It hid silently, this special college, in the shadow of a glacial erratic in the clammy center of Western Massachusetts. The campus was populated by strange children who ran barefoot through thickets and beech trees and spent their nights debating ideas they half-understood. RollsUponPrank should have revelled in the atmosphere, but she was too troubled to invest much effort into socializing.

The doctors at the school recommended that she have a pap smear, since she had never gotten one before. She obliged, begrudgingly, having no idea what it might entail.

There was a little room with watercolor flowers in glittery wire frames and a taupe chair that bent backwards with stirrups for her feet. When the doctor swished in and produced the speculum, a wave of fear gathered at her sex. And when he tried to push it inside her, her body acted first. She kicked him—*lightly*—in the face.

As a result, there was a therapist. She made the kind of encouraging small talk that precedes bad news. *Oh, you eat so healthy, all those almonds and carrots. You must do so much to care for your health.*

Then she angled her eyes, pained and sympathetic. "I think you have a repressed memory," she said, "and I think that you should consider therapy." RollsUponPrank understood the gist, but it didn't hit the part of her mind the therapist hoped—the part that feels an urgency about repairing things. She filed the information away and brought it up at awkward times, scaring her peers, and never presenting the issue to a professional.

The days shrunk down to a polar sliver, getting dark around 3pm. Each day she retreated to her room knowing there was something rotten at her core.

She practiced drawing dramatic eyeliner, styling her hair, and toning her body to distract from the corruption—the corruption that tangled her muscles and scattered her sense of identity.

It all cohered, she thought, as just one issue—resting in her sex and not her mind. Talking, she thought, was not enough to fix her. The gulf between her mind and body stretched too far across.

A Lonely King

Before Meta_king manifested his kingdom—when he was still in school, studying computers and money and all the different ways that numbers arrange themselves into reality—he was lonely.

He felt that girls didn't understand the power in his work, nor did they believe in his visions for the future. His peers were either intimidated or they struggled to keep pace with him. All this to say, Meta_king was alone on an expedition that no one cared about very much, and his plans drew yawns from those he'd hoped would join him.

Meta_king tried different experiments to become less lonely. He tried dancing, which was a sure way to get close to girls—and even to convince them to hold him tight. This was a definite source of pleasure, but too short lived; he had to find a way to make them stay.

He learned to play the guitar, and to play songs that were sad and romantic and jubilant. Still, he felt unwanted.

When he started to see girls showing up in his domain, the world of screens and numbers, it felt to him like an affront. How dare these girls come into this world that he had studied with the dedication of a king? And they had their hands out—not for *his* hand—but for money. He could barely handle the disgust.

With his education, it was no challenge for Meta_king to claim the data on their phones, computers, and tablets. It was easier still to make them stream and record at all times, unbeknownst to the owners. He knew the permissions on these devices made it all legitimate.

He started with RollsUponPrank; she suspected nothing—hadn't even asked for payment before his little show. With ease he set up a broadcast for her on a popular porn site. She carried her phone everywhere, and it saw her in the shower, on the toilet, choosing outfits, and even dancing like sweet milk on her modeling site. She had no idea why viewership was dwindling.

And so the girl collection was born. Slowly at first— just a few girls who had jilted him (or who had known him and had not approached) only to show up later, naked and begging. But the girl collection grew quickly, and in a backwards way, it helped him to carry the loneliness.

It was just an assemblage of images, images of abstracted flesh, membrane, cartilage. Unwittingly displayed in unending streams for the curious, the lonely, and even the spiteful. It gave Meta_king the sort of calloused attitude that surgeons get around gore. This was how he felt around girls now; their affections weren't as sweet, and their disinterest didn't sting so badly.

This, of course, is not a fitting attitude for a king.

Girl Collection

One of the great fighters of his time owned a strip club in Las Vegas, and it drew patrons from all around the world. It was called the Girl Collection.

RollsUponPrank took offense to the name whenever it was said that she should work there if she ever found herself out west, which happened surprisingly often. *Work at* Girl Collection? *No way.*

It was jarringly apt, which she typically liked. But she couldn't bring herself to say it aloud. So she never worked there, or in Las Vegas at all.

Though RollsUponPrank was already in a girl collection, and she was not getting paid. And this collection was rapidly growing: she was not the first nor the last girl Meta_king had chosen for the digital menagerie.

He had collected girls of very stripe and flavor, every manner, intellect, and taste. He had the heart of a king and the fingers of a boy, and he could not be satisfied until he had reviewed and angled each of these salacious avatars to his liking.

Being gracious, he had chosen to share the girl collection widely; it had become such an impressive taxonomy of the species that he could hardly claim it solely for himself and his friends. *This is how they do it on the west coast; this is how the blondes and redheads differ.* And so on.

These girls had no idea how precarious a position they had chosen—how exploitable they were. Meta_king was testing the boundaries of this problem, just as he had always done in school with other problems. And how sweet it felt to hold their fates in his royal hand, to treat them just as cavalierly as they did themselves.

As the girl collection grew, so did its popularity. Men from all over the world went to see what these creatures were doing under their veils of imagined privacy. They gazed in hysterical wonderment at their crudeness, their adorable moments, and their strange moods. It created a fearsome camaraderie among men, this secret to half the world.

Sometimes Meta_king would stay up at night and gaze into the screen of limbs and hair and teeth, of pink and brown and purple fleshy parts. Sometimes he would imagine that he knew the bodies, as lovers or sisters or colleagues.

Sometimes this flashed inside him involuntarily, and sometimes he truly *would* know a face. He would shake in disgust, partly with himself, and partly with women. The images became a morass of knowledge that was heavier against his brain each day.

Some of their abstracted parts thrashed under his eyes in the dark. A sphincter, a nostril. Then a whole face. He would blink harder and take a drink of warm water. He struggled this way sometimes until sleep found him under his indigo sheets in the night.

Wealth And The House

RollsUponPrank was always an orphan, though she had a family by blood. She had been raised in a house that felt haunted; drafty and echoing, with clanging pipes, and covered in such a volume of ivy that it looked somehow both blighted and imperious.

The family was very wealthy, though she didn't know exactly *how* wealthy, and the whole arrangement sounded quite idyllic to the untrained ear. There were two children, though they were quite troubled in the mind, and there were two parents of whom only one had a job. A lawyer. A powerful one at a historic firm, which had imposing bronze pillars in the lobby and a central office in downtown Pittsburgh.

One side of the family made their money bottling soda pop. On the other side, it was not clear where the money came from. But it all married together as you might expect, in a languid pool that didn't receive much and didn't offer much up. It was simply understood that it was there and must remain contained.

The family held fast to a fear of the unknown; perhaps it was an instinct toward containment for the pool of cash. RollsUponPrank wondered at this mysterious force at work. It could be cast in any direction at will, with deniability. Often times, it landed on her back.

Solace Online

In her family's dining room, there was a portrait of a man that RollsUponPrank had never heard of with a bullet hole straight through his canvas lip. The frame was burnished gold with impressions of flowers in its tracery. The story was that her grandfather got angry one day and shot it.

Her blood mother had grown up in a Honduran port town before sailing north to the states. She told stories about living there, spiders the size of your head and snakes that rustled low growth in the jungle. There was a rooster that would crow in the morning, and her father would scream at it. One day he threw a rock instead and shattered the window.

Her sense of personal history was gnarled up in threads like these. She was from a brutish and forceful people—but she couldn't square this with the careful way her family dealt with words. When they talked, they danced around the actual topic on their tiptoes like it might detonate. Things were just too dangerous to say directly. And so she became skilled at wordplay as if her health depended on it. At times, she felt as though it really did.

She was a blank girl, raised without manners, with no sense of history, and completely without a concept of sin. This typically made people look at her strangely (and sometimes with outright derision), and it stood to reason that the girl felt most at home online.

Magic And Religion

When RollsUponPrank was a child, she carefully approached her mother's room on her toes, clutching the door and hiding in the shadow slanted on her face. She had a crush. What could she do?

The mother never taught her about makeup or clothes or glamor. Instead she told her, "go down to the river and choose an armful of the smoothest stones. Then place them under your bed in a circle—cast your dreams of the boy right into the center."

She did as she was told; after school she took a bus headed south and crossed the iron tracks to wander on the bank of the Monongahela. She found a hidden path down from the rocky cliff lined with decoratively-arranged bricks, laid there by vagabonds. She tiptoed down through the tunnel in the hillside thicket and found herself at the bank, with the evidence of campsites in 40 oz bottles and neon plastic bags. She also found a wealth of stones, and little bits of smoothed glass. She remembered she was only there for the stones; she filled her pockets with the glossiest, most sparkling specimens. And when she was almost too heavy with rocks, she made her way back up.

When night fell, she arranged them underneath her bed and cast her wish.

RollsUponPrank grew up with a sense that the spirit world was a mass of all-purpose solutions. She applied the poultice of some witch craft or another to nearly every problem in her life. She found it mystifying, and sort of hilarious, that some people were offended by magic. Still, she never called herself a witch. But only because she found that corny—it was a far more vigorous thing, she thought, to be accused or even just suspected.

RollsUponPrank is the closest you will find to a witch in this story; she's also the closest you'd find to a witch in your own life, unless you live a very unusual life indeed.

Father

RollsUponPrank also had a father by blood; this father required constant tending, but he couldn't offer up much in return except for occasional flat and silky dollars, uncrumpled by other peoples' hands. He stayed up all night drinking red wine and listening to metal, and when he was around during the day, he sat in one place on the couch that grew a dent and let cans gather around him for the women to clean up.

He never had much to say to RollsUponPrank, but sometimes she would hear him in a rumbling register when he thought she was sleeping on the couch, "she is so beautiful," or "it really seems she gets more pretty all the time." She felt something leaden perched on her chest, holding her down. She wouldn't stir.

RollsUponPrank felt herself in two parts, marbled together like fat and flesh. One part needed to feel beautiful, the other could not handle being seen. She learned to shelter that slippery part with masks.

She carefully built up her look from her sun-red hair to her porcelain feet, so that no one's eyes could ever quite catch her. She lamented that this game has no champion and no ending.

So RollsUponPrank split her attention between studies and the craft of sparkling masks of distraction. She performed well in school, but the confusion kept her from pursuing anything that would earn her respect.

Woodworking

The grandfather—the one who beamed a rooster with a rock because it crowed—held an unsettling smile over his forceful mien, like a dramaturgy mask. His wife described it as *gravitas*. He expected people to do as he said, and smile back. And when they didn't, he switched masks. It made sense to RollsUponPrank; she knew about masks.

He spoke out from under his fedora—always the fedora, no need for a reason. He wore it in the house and even in the woodworking station in the basement.

RollsUponPrank and her sister would visit the grandparents and go to the basement, following the crude staircase with the effluvium of sawdust dancing under a single stringed bulb, inventing tiny colors in the sphere of illumination.

One year the sister had crutches—an offense to his strength. The grandfather had a plan, he held it tightly under the lip of his hat. He told the children to follow him down to the basement. Curlicues of pale shaved wood nestled in the braid rug.

He pulled an axe off the pine pegs in the wall and chopped the crutches into little blocks, then threw them in a pile in the corner. He told them to build her a cane.

Her noodly freckled arms were no good for sawing, so she chose a pre-cut piece of small wood and hammered it frightfully to a larger one. The nail stuck out to make it look like a weapon. She held it between her knees and brought the hammer far above her head, and flinched every time it made contact.

They painted it purple and green, with polka dots. The sister used it for months until she healed. RollsUponPrank wore her mask of compliance.

Escape

RollsUponPrank tried desperately to escape from the family, but their vast resources ensnared her like devouring vines and the men had unspoken motives to keep her close at hand. She felt that the love of another man was her only path outward.

She clung to her fantasy like wet hard plastic. She would find refuge in somebody strange, and they would live near the ocean's dramatic stew, and she could tell tales and he could tend to his kingdom. She tried to create this life again and again, dreaming up love with nearly anyone who would take her. Friends watched her suffer and said *hell, maybe try therapy.*

Escape was her primary goal when she went to school—it ranked above her studies. She prayed to meet a boy so they could start a new family without noxious obligations or confusing judgements. Instead, she found herself thwarted by the corruption in her sex. It meant she couldn't share herself with anyone, despite her most creative attempts.

The corruption lived in the very center of her body, but it shone outwardly as a social flaw. A sudden prudishness stemming a performance of sexuality. Her body screeched *no* and her limbs locked up with fear before the act had even opened, and she would kick the boy out of her room with an urgency she later saw as quite insensitive.

Part of her held on to faith that she would find her king and they would escape together. Over time, her dream wicked down to almost nothing—she merely wanted someone who was patient while she untangled her sex. It proved to be her greatest obstacle.

Problem Solving

Her body was the answer, RollsUponPrank believed. She would force her body to comply with sex. Her mind contained too many minds within it—she would surely die before she managed to unwind them. And anyway, that confusion was so much worse than any discomfort from sexual exploration— or maybe it was just problem solving. So she started at the lips of her sex and not in a therapist's chair.

She did some research online and discovered that you can tame the condition with dilators, like rounded and cylindrical matryoshka dolls you slide inside your sex, sneaky-like, incrementally sizing up. They can start as small as a q-tip. She started right away—she ordered a set of them online from a company with an unlikely name so that the family wouldn't suspect what she was up to.

She didn't feel any shame about sex—only about her condition. So when she laid on the smooth white tile of the locked bathroom with the discomfort of plastic against her tense innermost muscle, she felt more impatient than anything else.

She didn't understand that pleasure was the way to ease the tension; she was just a girl, after all. To her, sex was just a central part of the escape plan—it held no intrinsic magic.

Her older boyfriend at the time was unsympathetic to her slow progress. "I'm not in high school," he warned her, "I have expectations." So she sought something more powerful to hasten her work.

Soon, she discovered alcohol as an assistive tool. It allowed her to make wonderful progress, and soon she was having uninhibited sex, and was fully desensitized to the appearance of sex toys.

Her parents didn't bother to hide alcohol in the home, and it was always around at the boyfriend's house. Besides, she worked at a restaurant and the bartender was always happy to ply her with something, being a young girl amused by his craft.

Lying

RollsUponPrank often struggled with the truth. That's a gentle way to say it. She thought most writers were like that, turning real life into stories, always seeing the potential in everyday events. As she moved through life, she came to understand that this trait pissed people off, and that many writers actually confine their fictionalizations to the page— especially those writers that don't drink very much.

RollsUponPrank was still twisted up inside—although she had successfully opened her sex— and she couldn't quite make out what the problem was. So she took stabs at it, and they were often close, but horrifying. Especially when she drank, she sometimes made a scene with brutal pronouncements to which no one could respond. *She had been raped! As a child! There were predators everywhere! Nothing would ever be okay!*

She had no way of consulting her own memory to be sure. But she had a deep inner sense of wrongness that could only be conveyed through ludicrous intoxication. Others could see that her problem was foundational, or nearly so, and they rarely tried to intervene. Nothing they could do would hit her that deep. People chose to either make fun of her or walk away; it was much simpler that way. She could hardly blame them.

RollsUponPrank didn't realize what a reputation she had earned for lying, and she had nothing to say for herself when called on it. People were right to question the veracity of anything she said. She often felt her words had no value beyond entertainment. This only solidified her self-concept as a whore, and consequently, upheld the sense of wrongness in her sex-mind.

High School

RollsUponPrank went to high school in the wet slate city center of Pittsburgh. This school sat in between a strip club and a grand convention center. Sometimes, when she and her friends smoked cigarettes in the alley after school, the purveyor of the club would linger on RollsUponPrank. *Come on, let's get you back on stage.* She was wearing the bag of a schoolgirl, and could never tell if he actually mistook her for a dancer or if he was simply toying with her mind.

The school was narrow and seven stories tall. The line for the metal detectors wound around the block, past the strip club and a pub that specialized in chipped meats, and a nocturnal underground dance hall called the Pegasus. It took her maybe an hour to get through the line into school, but it was usually just a show. Often she noticed the detectors weren't plugged in.

Aron

The first time that RollsUponPrank met Aron, he was hunched in the alley between the club and the school. He was eating a bag of sour candy, one color at a time. He ate all the red pieces, then puked. Then he ate all the yellow pieces and puked again. He continued until there was a gummy rainbow on the pavement. He stood proudly at the vertex.

Every year there was a special convention in the city, one for adults who dress up like cartoon animals to have sex. The furry convention. Whenever it rolled into town all of the students took note of whoever was absent, with comic suspicion.

One year, it lined up with the rifle convention, and Aron snuck in with RollsUponPrank. They took pictures of him posing with a crew of grown men dressed as cats and bunnies and panthers, all wielding massive semi-automatic rifles. Aron kneeled in the center holding up peace signs.

It didn't take very long for Aron to get expelled from school. If it wasn't the knife from his nighttime job with the postal service, it would have been the drugs or the truancy. Eventually, an officer seized the blade from his back pocket during a rare thorough search.The administration promptly kicked him out, making the bad boy finish his diploma in a room they set up inside of an abandoned mall.

Meanwhile, RollsUponPrank wore her mask of compliance and made it through to an early graduation.

By the time Aron was going to mall school, he had taken a job in a gritty little sex shop out toward the country. There were personal booths in the back where men could watch movies and stroke themselves in relative privacy; Aron's job was to clean up those booths.

They would laugh at the nasty props he found—greasy rubber chickens and rubber gloves and balloons and high heels. She imagined in her child's mind the ways they factored into sex.

John Hammer Square

By this time, the truth was unavoidable—RollsUponPrank was quite strange. Jokes did not come easily with her peers, her reference material was just too creepy. She only felt the sweet comfort of kinship with strangelings, most of whom were several years her senior.

Aron and RollsUponPrank had the same affliction, and they both became frequent visitors of a certain house on John Hammer Square, a tight dead-end street near the college where troupes of strange artists would roll through and spend the night. These odd creators marvelled at the worldly children with no worried parents to scold them or carry them home.

The house was a leaky shotgun with talkative floor panels and a faded maroon facade. In storms it threatened to blow away. The front door would open without a key if you shook it hard enough—a feature much appreciated by anyone who needed a place to sleep late at night with a dead phone.

There was a rotating cast of odd children at John Hammer Square, mostly girls. She would have been anonymous except that she was dating the lessor.

Crow's Eyes

Crow's Eyes, a caravan of noise artists, liked the childrens' stories the most. The group would sit in the busted basement with string lights pinned up along the rotted beams. Aron and RollsUponPrank would tell tales while the group laughed incredulously at the stupid and dangerous lives they lived in the city.

Aron would tell tales about mall school, or about beer enemas, or about cooking scallops in storage units, and sometimes the artists would produce field recorders to capture his tales.

Noise filled the home with fellow strange creators who flew in from Sydney, or from Essex, or from Virginia Beach. Sometimes they were kind and curious, and sometimes they tried to ply the children with opiates. Only Aron took any.

If it wasn't for his iron constitution, the pretty boy probably would have died by age eighteen. Everyone was charmed by his acrobatic dance with a truly humiliating death. *Would he or wouldn't he?* Everyone except the little girls, who cared too much.

Ravensbeak

One of those noise nights was special. Ravensbeak had flown in from Australia, and everyone went to see the bloody spectacle. He would play sheet glass—with his *face!*—by affixing contact microphones to it and then lubricating the surface with petroleum jelly. It would break apart throughout the show and leave him striped and bloody.

Ravensbeak was slated to play at The Nerve. This was an abandoned fieldhouse that sat on the same property as the public pool. Noise artists would take it over in the off-seasons, and set up elaborate metal installations and other structures of trash that changed the acoustics of the open box to confuse and stun with sound. They looked like monuments on the moon.

The night of Ravensbeak's show, RollsUponPrank's boyfriend had torched her heart—in one of the ways any person of experience has witnessed between older men and young girls. He had ignored her calls, or sat with another girl at a show, or some such thing.

Whatever it was exactly that drew blood, RollsUponPrank could not bring herself to go inside and watch Ravensbeak play himself to strips. Instead, the jilted girl sat and drank vodka from a plastic bottle right on the sidewalk in front of The Nerve.

As much as RollsUponPrank loved The Nerve, she loved her boyfriend more than that, and it only got worse the meaner he was to her. She viewed his dismissiveness as a vigorous trial on her path to freedom. In truth, of course, it was rather unimportant.

Around this time, she stopped seeing Aron around; last she heard, he had designs to rob a pharmacy.

Whores

RollsUponPrank was often perceived as a whore; she didn't take it as an insult, but she could never pinpoint why people saw this quality in her—it wasn't only men—and she figured that they were correct.

She had entered adulthood and left for Chicago, partly to escape her family and partly to escape all the reminders of her ex boyfriend, which seemed to stain everything in Pittsburgh. As she walked from the train to her La Villita apartment, old ladies would call out to her from their windows. "What are you doing out here? Just walking around?"

In the same tone, men would pull over and roll down their car windows to ask if she wanted to get inside. When she said no, they just stared at her dumb for a moment. "Are you sure?" They would ask, as in, *are you sure you aren't out here selling it?*

It never occurred to RollsUponPrank that this was a bad thing to be. She knew that it was uncomfortable—the public is not sympathetic to whores, and whores have no recourse for their pain—but whoring seemed like the fastest route to get the unvarnished truth out of a person. Like an iron ore vein running cold and raw beneath polite society. She saw it in Aron. She felt it herself, at times.

Besides, whores were always kindest to RollsUponPrank. She had easily befriended the whores on her block; they told her where to find loose cigarettes and helped her evaluate outfits. When strange men stumbled out of El Grito Desesperado #2, a community center for addicts, the whores were the only ones to help them find their way.

If all of life was a game, and there were whores and squares, It seemed that the squares were ostensibly winning but the whores had heart, and that was more important. This was her attitude.

Choked Out

RollsUponPrank broke into a vast and private shelter as she crumpled to the stained wood floor, dissolving in grey static. Each step of her fall folded out into a crude animation. She felt many parts of herself shuffle into each slide. Only a few of them registered the potted fern that broke against the ground under her head. She awoke with soil in her nostrils and a flat drone in her head.

Her new boyfriend, Jonathan, had choked her out cold. He was the first, though not the last, to do this. She met him on FetLife, a fetish dating hub.

As the choking started, she felt a certain twinge in her core—somewhere deeper than the muscle, somewhere seated in her viscera. But it was illegible to her mind. She thought that he was posing a challenge, and she refused to tap out. She preferred to suffer physical harm than rejection, even the mere potential of rejection.

Fetish Dating

RollsUponPrank had become very fluent with her masks. She could pretend to be any sort of girl having any genre of experience—whatever would earn her a flicker of sexual praise. By now she had graduated from simple masks to full-bodied disguises. She could shed the problems in her mind if she simply refused to claim them, she thought, if she simply adopted the persona of somebody different.

She couldn't practice this skill in the world of traditional dating. Those relationships posed the danger of progression, which would require her to reveal such simple facts as the place of her birth, the names of her parents, and so on. And so the girl sought out strangelings in the fetish underground. This allowed her to practice her brand of naked pretending.

She invented an entirely new woman, and embodied her. This fictive woman was Jonathan's girl. He never really knew RollsUponPrank. And she never knew him.

This man had branded himself as an expert in the art of tying knots. Sometimes, when another man would strike up a conversation with him in a bar, he would show off his own girl collection of knotted up women, suspended or kneeling on the ground below his camera.

Sometimes, as she worked on her webcam modeling, he would stylize his posture in the background. Not playing with himself or anything that would demonstrate investment, but posing with a quiet, firm, and studying gaze. Wearing a mask of his own.

Not Once, But Thrice

RollsUponPrank knew that her interior wrongness had gone terminal when she got fired—for the third time—from the strip club. She didn't know anyone who had even been fired *once*, but she comforted herself with the thought that she worked at *gentlemen's clubs* with *champagne rooms* and not at dives. Though it was likely that if she had worked at a dive, she would have manufactured unforgivable problems there, too.

It wasn't clear if this meant she wasn't a stripper at all, or if it meant that she was the worst stripper of all time.

The first time she got fired was at VIPs. This was the main gentlemen's club in Chicago that actually served alcohol, and it operated under mafioso-style management that might seem charming and peculiar to the uninitiated. The managers had found a loophole in the city's mandate that any club with topless dancers could not serve alcohol.

Rather than simply become a juice bar and attract patrons too young to bring any money, they implemented a system whereby the girls would paint their nipples with flesh-toned liquid latex (from their own coffers, of course), and have their picture taken before and after each shift to demonstrate that their legally private parts were sufficiently covered.

She wondered how long the club held on to those photos, and how they sorted them. She knew they used dated, physical copies. But when she got a letter in the mail years later about a class-action lawsuit against the club's shell company, she imagined that it wasn't organized so well after all; maybe the boys just thumbed through them on long nights and made jokes about the dancers. That was what she usually pictured them doing anyway.

Pediatric Cardiologist

The first night that RollsUponPrank got fired, the club had started plying the girls with free flutes of champagne, walked around the club by black suited men on matte black trays. There was a medical conference in the city, and the lobby was full of surgeons and dermatologists and doctors-to-be, and the girls were not excited enough for the men.

She was already alienating herself because she didn't know the subtleties of table dances between clubs. At VIPs, there was no contact allowed—certainly no friction. But that was the only type of dance she had ever seen. So she tried it on a (very pleased) general practitioner.

Management tried to call her to the back over the loudspeaker, but she had already forgotten the name she had chosen for herself. (Mona, "Like Mona Lisa?" "Your words, not mine"). When the general manager asked if she was stupid or something, all she could say was "Yes, I am. I'm sorry." This surprised him so much that he actually apologized—"No you aren't, sweetheart." And so she went back out on the floor.

She ended up selling a champagne room to a pediatric cardiologist with tragic eyes and went on to get completely wrecked, to his delight. First he ordered champagne, and when her wig fell off and she didn't care, he took that as a sign to order a bottle of vodka. The two would alternate swigs from the bottle and share war stories; his tales had more color, since they had actual dead babies with heart conditions.

Soon enough, RollsUponPrank blacked out—the last she could remember was stumbling upstairs to the dressing room and texting some friends for help. She came back another night to see if they would let her dance again, to no avail. She had written out a treatise in her defense in pink marker. She thought they might find it endearing. Probably some of them did—the few that enjoyed her antics.

Polecats

RollsUponPrank was fired, once again, from Polecats. She struggled with blacking out in champagne rooms, where there was relative privacy, access to an entire bottle of something, and a man who desperately wanted her to lose herself.

She had done just that on her very first night. She listened to the house mom's introduction, and memorized the prices for champagne rooms by repeating them out loud to herself as she swaggered around on the floor—in a casual way, not like a vulture. She sold a champagne room right away to a friendly older gentleman in a golf shirt (the mark of a prospect, she knew by then).

While they were together, she got destroyed on some red liquid, then a clear one. She couldn't remember how she got out of the room, or the club, or back home that night. When she came back the next day to pick up the remainder of her earnings—what she didn't wake up to find folded in her garter—she was summarily told she should never come back.

And when she went to the Gold Club to see if they would have her, they wouldn't even let her re-audition. They had started with the usual pleasantries—*Nice to see you again! Where have you been, Mona? We missed you*—but she didn't have the good sense to lie about her predicament, or even the knowledge that it was shameful. So when the manager asked her why she wasn't at VIPs anymore, she told him straight that it was because she's an alcoholic.

MetaStage

By this time, Meta_king had found great success beyond the girl collection. He was not so lonely anymore—wealth carries with it a chest of short-lived affections—and his calloused attitude toward women had expanded to include most men. It seemed that people largely wanted something from him, with no interest in repayment. At worst, they wanted to fool him into giving something up.

He thought back often to that moment with RollsUponPrank, who asked him straightforwardly why he chose to lie. He wasn't used to that sort of candor then or now. It was funny, he thought, how often he found himself repeating her words. Not to anyone in particular, but to himself, just under his breath, as he walked away.

Sometimes Meta_king checked the girl collection to watch RollsUponPrank stumbling through life on her drunken, high-heeled feet. He watched her carve names into candles and gather plants on some phase of the moon or other. He wondered what she was trying to achieve, and if she would ever find out that she was a collectible.

He knew she wasn't simply stupid. He heard her speak at school, and he knew that she could write, and he had spied her composing screeds that would absolutely shrivel the skin on a weaker man like icy water. He wondered if she would take the heels off and notice that she was a writer.

And while she struggled, Meta_king elevated his friends to a techy brand of courtly success. The group had the feel of a secret society. Nobody outside their group knew exactly what they did, but their incredible sway in the digital realm was widely known. The group carried all the evidence of wealth amassed quickly.

Meta_king's company, MetaStage, dealt with data. This meant that they dealt with everything. Sounds, the root pain of cold on a tooth, the heft of a garfish on a child's rod, all of this could be observed and represented as auditory or haptic data. Entire human girls, even: the rhythms of their days, the ways they cleaned themselves or stayed dirty, the stability of their relationships. All of this could be captured and manipulated by Meta_king.

With such an expansive range of subjects, his kingdom was vast and opulent, and most of all, secret. And in the case of certain subjects, like the girl collection, that was absolutely for the best. If it were to become public knowledge—that is, public not just to curious men—surely there would be outrage at how much he owned, how much he *knew*.

Real Names

Between dancing at clubs, creating pornography, and generally floating from city to city and clique to clique, RollsUponPrank had gone several years without the people closest to her knowing her real name. They called her by her stripper name, or her online handle (which was RollsUponPrank, of course). That didn't bother her much, but it was jarring when she would hear her birth name.

It was especially eerie to hear the most formal version of her name, the one that nobody had ever called her casually. And this was the version of her name that she heard the most, because it would only come out for something essential, like signing a document, or requesting payment. It summoned static at her neck; it was never spoken in times of peace, only in times of demand, and sometimes to cause deliberate discomfort.

RollsUponPrank never accepted her birth name as her own. Perhaps because she lived in such a different world than the parents who gave it. She lived in the underworld, especially the digital one, and she lived amongst peers who understood her perfectly or not at all.

Meta_king was not shy about his real name, but it was often irrelevant in his work. He had to use traceless techniques to avoid revealing his secrets, like a wizard hiding his ability from the wary public.

And Meta_king did have special powers: he could manipulate the appearance of anything online, change numbers around, alter text to make it seem as though it had always looked a certain way. This is to say, he could arrange reality however he wanted it. And it wasn't because his company had amassed so much money—though they had—it was because of his personal skill.

Privacy was the best way for him to avoid arousing suspicion or fear from the public. Those emotions tend to spread among people like rot.

And so it was that RollsUponPrank was fully exposed online, but few people in life knew her deeply. Meta_king was undetectable online, but served as the smiling figurehead of a powerful company. Both felt uniquely unseen.

Angry Missives

RollsUponPrank moved to New Orleans on a lark shortly after a vaccine became available for the corona virus. She had cloistered herself through the contagious event in a Chicago studio where she worked remotely, furiously typing legal briefs at a high volume for a greedy international employer. She still held fast to her heart her romantic dreams of escape—the pace of her work and the effort to build a career had done nothing to change her priorities.

The distinction between day and night ceased to matter, her connection to the world had waned down to a sharp and painful sickle, and she started drinking in the mornings. It helped her write, at first. And then she started firing off missives to people who had wronged her, which was her wont even when sober.

RollsUponPrank had already become the sort of person who says things that other people only think. So when she set out to make someone see her perspective, she often went ten layers too deep without realizing she even hit her mark.

Typically she did this to men, men she had dated who had caused her pain. It took her years on average to realize that she had been hurt (she had to remove her mask before she could triage the pain). These men never wanted to hear about it, not even for a fight—they had already moved on. Sometimes they assumed a posture of greater emotional maturity, which shook her with anger.

There were no boundaries she would not cross, verbally. Illness, poverty, fitness, talent—she would rake her forked tongue across it all. Her phone hosted a graveyard of blocked numbers.

Moving to New Orleans

New Orleans seemed like a good fit for RollsUponPrank. She had heard that a certain type of freedom was possible there that other places tried to kill with city planning and police forces and collective values. It seemed to have a general shamelessness and an appreciation for the unseen world that snagged in the gears of midwestern pragmatism. So she anxiously made her plans, packed her things, and set out for the deep south.

RollsUponPrank had packed her things into a steel pod that parked in her alley, and she booked a smaller steel pod to sleep in on the train. She had never traveled by train and found it incredibly romantic, watching the flat midwestern countryside slide into the south, which unfurled in pink ruffles of crepe myrtle. She drank in the diner car with a group of old college friends traveling for a wedding party. All of them were fascinated by her impulsivity and frank speech—she gave them a sense of local flavor, though she was not local.

When she stepped off the train, she surveyed the palm trees and relative quiet of the midday station. It seemed impossible to her that palm trees could grow naturally anywhere—and it was true, the trees were imported. It was right that the landscape felt to her so warm and uncanny.

The Borgias

When RollsUponPrank worked for that firm in Chicago—the one that had her up inside the black morning writing briefs, catching pennies in a hat for the labor—and before she started working from home because of the pandemic, she went into an office every day in one of those austere towers of Chicago.

She took an elevator all the way up to the top, in a room that looked out over the golden crested buildings and chrome sculptures with the bay of the great lake mirrored in their curves. There, she wrote at a desk next to a boy just her age. The two of them would commiserate about the job and trade jokes. Their conversations had an urgent ring that gave her hope of romantic escape, her still-persisting dream.

Sometimes she would visit his apartment by the sports stadium. By the time they were close enough for him to come visit her apartment, something in his demeanor had changed.

He had a voice much bigger than whatever room contained it. She chalked it up to his years in theater; apparently he acted in college, and it seemed like he worked to keep those skills firm. But even when the two were completely alone in her room, he would shoot out his voice in a ballistic way—to graze someone else's ear, and not hers. She thought he might be trying to impress her roommate in some show of masculinity.

RollsUponPrank attempted to bond despite the slight, unattributed tension. She hadn't yet enjoyed a schoolgirl romance. She showed him parts of her journal, shared her favorite songs and pontificated on their greatness.

One sad song perked up his ears.

"Do you know what this song's about?" He asked, as though he was putting the question before a vast audience.

"No, like, I guess it's about power?"

"Do you know about the Borgias?" he asked her.

She did not. But she sat dutifully and listened as he explained their strategy of holding onto power through inbreeding. He looked at RollsUponPrank as if he expected her to have thoughts prepared.

Something about siblings together, and fathers and daughters, all overheated her mind like a black stone in the sun. She couldn't take it. She turned the music off.

She did not know that he was shooting out his voice to graze her phone.

Hurricane Preparation

RollsUponPrank's apartment—the camelback of a shotgun house—peered out behind a soft jungle of ferns, elephant ears, and mondo grass, only showing its speckled greige lid and attic windows, like cartoon eyes. She used to open the front and back doors when it rained to watch the lizards and roaches run so slippery outside, forming their own traffic patterns on the sidewalks. It felt almost like camping.

The fridge, air conditioner, and stove top only worked occasionally. The support beams under the ceiling's a-frame were burned to a black, bubbly crisp—and ironically, there was no smoke alarm. The street glowed like lava at night with wavering gas lamps on each of her neighbors' doorways.

She had timed her move for hurricane season, and she found herself woefully unprepared. By way of supplies, her apartment came equipped with a cowbell and a broken flashlight. She did precisely nothing to protect the structure from the oncoming storm. In fact, she left a couple windows slightly open by accident.

People around her tittered about storm categories and projected wind speeds. The girl couldn't wrap her mind around all that data. She only cared about the time of landfall. Aside from that, everything could pivot in a simple instant, and it would be too late to reverse your decision to stay or go.

RollsUponPrank spied on her neighbors to the right—it wasn't hard, the windows faced each other, naked, and the walls were thin as foil. The children had come to check on their grandparents' plans. The grandmother lifted up her arms from the cot where she was resting, surrounded by tissues and cat toys and printer paper. "You'll hafta drag me outta here kickin and screamin!" She just felt too old to run. That seemed to be a popular judgement, even with the young.

Anthony

RollsUponPrank had surprised herself that she could hold a traditional job. Having learned that, she suspected she could do a traditional relationship, too. And with zero local connections and dwindling funds, it seemed like the fastest way to access fun and information.

It didn't take much to impress the girl—she was used to testing her masks, as though she had something massive to prove. And dating in New Orleans is a famously low-effort jaunt. So when Anthony messaged her to recommend that she leave for the coming storm, it felt like an act of romantic heroism.

Anthony didn't say much, which she took as a sign of intelligent restraint instead of pride. He was only a year her senior, stood a full head above her, and trained as a fighter in his off hours. Most compellingly, he worked as an engineer at the nuclear plant making a comfortable salary. It looked like a bottle cap on a map, but it held enough power to destroy the entire state, and maybe more. It must take a quiet mind to manage such volatile materials, she thought.

As she crouched on the ground in her evacuation hotel room, drunk and shivering, he propped her up with links to guide her through the storm—maps of the city's power grid, illuminating streets with power in a validating green; crowdsourced maps of businesses that were still active; and so on. It steadied her breathing.

When the two could finally meet for a date, Anthony was just as reticent to share his thoughts as ever. But RollsUponPrank didn't mind; she was drawn to his simplicity, his lack of neurosis, and his willingness to do the uninteresting tasks of life that must be done.

After all, with her array of masks, she could easily conjure romance where there was none.

Houston

RollsUponPrank's neighbor dropped her off in Houston—he banged on her door at the last possible moment to ask if she had an escape plan. She carried the pink and black cloth duffel she used to bring to the strip club, filled frantically with her teal toothbrush and whatever weather-appropriate clothes she imagined she might need, which turned out to be mostly rags and mens' boxers and sweatpants. She had no idea what the Texas sun would do to the rain.

She checked into a room at the first motel she found, which was almost full; of course, everyone else from New Orleans was trying to escape as well. But she did manage to get a room. On payment she felt the sting of hurricane inflation—but not that acutely through the rime of alcohol, amphetamines, and adrenaline that encrusted her.

She spent her days camped out with a book at the bar across the street. Girls in orange booty shorts and doll-sized tank tops carried jewel colored glass hookahs with burning fruits on their crowns. The room was full of stage vapor, even at 10am, and pitchers of tangerine colored mixed drinks were slung around the bar all morning. They never kicked her out for staying half the day.

As she walked from the hotel to the gas station for a bottle of anything, a car pulled up next to her, asking if she wanted to get inside. She wondered at the fact that this seemed to happen to her no matter the region and no matter her age. She wondered if this happened to other girls too—

certainly not at the same rate, but at least once in a while—or if it was a facet of her personal wrongness.

RollsUponPrank did have an easy manner about her; she carried all of her things on her back, and she wore all of her jewelry in a careless tangle around her neck, that looked somewhat expensive and not particularly well cared for. She wore shirts that only reached halfway down her torso, exposing her colorful traditional tattoos in notoriously painful locations, and her pants were baggy, as though they had been borrowed from a man (and they likely had been).

She at least looked like a traveler, one who would sleep anywhere and wake up looking more-or-less the same, and maybe that was the same thing as a whore, she thought, not lingering on the question for too long. There was not much that she could do to build a new persona from scratch; this one had been cobbled together from a lifetime of ease and hardship in the right places.

Dr. Gwendolyn

When RollsUponPrank made it back to her room that sweaty cobalt night, she knew she had to deal with the money problem. She had no job or prospects; she needed cheaper lodging to ride out the storm. A few swipes on her phone and she found a budget spot owned by a woman named Dr. Gwendolyn.

She got ready to move. By this I mean, she hosed herself down with cold water in the shower to dampen the alcoholic rosacea, and re-reddened her cheeks and lips with rose tinted balm. She half-appraised herself: surprisingly healthy, if not slightly puffed. But her giant red hair masked that in her face, or at least complemented it.

Then she went about gathering and disposing of the bottles, of which there were at least a dozen in different sizes, colors, and materials—the gas station didn't carry a steady supply of anything she liked too much.

Dr. Gwendolyn was a strange woman—something of a witch herself—who smiled unnervingly wide as she spoke and who refused to let you leave a conversation. She was an elbow-gripper. RollsUponPrank barely noticed and was only half-lucid, creating a hilarious interplay that neither party could appreciate.

The woman's home was full of altars—money altars in the fireplace, filled with framed pictures of herself and her diplomas, and artfully folded bills to create pop-up houses, swans, and flowers. She had laminated photos of mansions and castles strewn about the home under ornate metal paperweights as if they were places she visited often, or that she was considering for purchase. She told stories about those places, and from her eyes alone the girl could tell they were lies.

When RollsUponPrank showered, Dr. Gwendolyn would walk straight into the gleaming white bathroom and look her in the eyes as she spoke, through the nakedness. She was almost too shocked to ask the host to leave.

When her door was locked, the woman shook the knob and knocked. It was too much. She had to leave. In the interim, she holed herself up in the room drinking, watching the electrical grid map closely until it told her that she was safe to go home.

The very minute she saw that line on her side of the street had flipped from red to green, she bought a ticket. The soonest one departed at midnight, but all the better; she wouldn't have to say goodbye to Dr. Gwendolyn, and she would claim an aisle to sleep through the ride.

Return Home

When RollsUponPrank got off the bus on Canal street at the start of the red streetcar line, she was stunned at how dead it all was. Banana trees dramatically folded over, soft stalked plants all bereft and prone, all the shops boarded up and empty. Everything slicked down grey. She wondered if the strip would ever recover.

She ordered a car home and saw that the plants around her house were suffering the same affliction, but the inside of her camelback room was totally untouched, even though she left in such a hurry that there were two windows open—*two*!

Of course, everything inside the fridge smelled like wet rot, but fortunately there were only a couple of items in there anyway, so she had no need to trash the entire appliance, which people sometimes have to do. Once she threw those out and closed the windows, the ascent to normalcy began; the mourning plants perked back up, and the businesses on Canal street opened back up, and the streetcars got to running just like they always do.

Bad Trick

In all her years of being mistaken for a whore—or maybe being judged correctly, but not liking it—RollsUponPrank developed a trick to stay the accusations. When men approached in their cars and asked if she wanted a ride, she wore her mask of disinterest and said "No, I'm a fed."

Usually they wouldn't offer more by way of protest than a skeptical eyebrow and an upward inflected, "For real?" to which she would say, "For real." The man would either peel off or get a look that said, "Damn, this neighborhood has changed."

Sometimes RollsUponPrank had to use this technique on foot, which was decidedly less comfortable for her, because she had to account for someone looking *her* closely in the eyes for too long and having discernment for these things. RollsUponPrank did not carry herself like a cop, and her mask of authority was not very strong.

One day, she was at the grocery getting her usual bottle of whatever and something to eat, and a man approached asking if she wanted to hang out, and how much might it cost. She was quick that day, and said, "actually, I'm a cop. We can talk more if you want."

She evaluated his eyes. He was just an older man with no desire for a fight, and he seemed like he would have treated her nicely enough if she had actually taken him up on it. Of course, the demeanor beforehand is no way to judge safety or kindness after the act. Even most square women know that (not that RollsUponPrank actually considered bedding the stranger).

Later, as she walked down Magazine Street in a sweet and aimless way, just taking in the fruits and trees and strange birds with subtropical voices, another man approached, younger this time. He pointed to her scales tattoo, loud and traditional on her shoulder. "Are you a libra?"

RollsUponPrank acted too quickly on instinct. "No, I'm a fed." The exchange went on as usual. "Damn, for real?" "For real." And he hurried off around the back of Rainbow Grocery, where she assumed he was telling his friends about the whore fed.

What she didn't account for was that she had very identifiable markings, and his friends took accusations of that nature very seriously. Before too long, RollsUponPrank had a reputation in her own neighborhood as the enemy. This, of course, was never her goal.

Fed Mask

When RollsUponPrank returned from her evacuation to Houston, everything was broken and oblique for weeks before the city fell back in the pocket again.

Word had spread throughout her neighborhood that RollsUponPrank was a spy. And while many neighbors watched her suspiciously, some of them extended her a hesitant welcome.

The couple across the street had seen firsthand that the girl was not fit for spying—she needed to be blasted to accomplish anything. These types are not terribly uncommon in New Orleans, and they do not pose a threat so long as they are plied properly with the correct substances and checked on every so often.

The couple offered her beer they had been gifted from the neighborhood brewery to drink before it went bad through the storm. The girl spent her days on their porch and in the bed of their truck smoking marijuana. She felt at peace in their home on the lip of the river's crescent.

Other neighbors had given RollsUponPrank a welcoming hand. One group was working on a cinderblock structure that got busted up in the storm. It had been a grey block on the corner and now it stood—or rested, as it were—as a ruined grey pile. The group would grill under a plastic tarp in the rain and deliberate on how to get it fixed up correctly, and cheap.

One day they noticed RollsUponPrank. They had heard that she was a spy, but didn't believe the rumors. Still, they could acknowledge that she had the look. They offered her some red drink from the cooler and invited her to chat.

They told her that another man had been collecting federal money for *their* building all the way back from a different storm, and the agency had never bothered to verify the owner. "You look like you work for them," they told her, "want to help us give him a scare?"

RollsUponPrank said "Of *course*." She loved pranks, and she loved secret missions more. So she showed them her leather portfolio and put on the reflective orange vest they gave her. "Look at her. She looks just like a fed. She's perfect!"

She approached the neighbor's house and asked the questions they supplied her with. She knocked in five bursts of three until he answered—a fat and serious man in an apologetic white tank who indulged her line of questions without much to say.

Her mask of authority had failed; it was stilted and awkward, and she wasn't able to extract anything useful. Still, her new friends liked her gamesmanship and offered to boil crawfish in her yard next week.

Neighbor Or Spy?

The spy rumors came around to get RollsUponPrank; this is the trouble with masks, or the trouble with never taking them off. No one can vouch for the wearer, not knowing what lives underneath.

One night her neighbors were having a party. Not her friends, but in the house next to theirs, across from one that was torn down completely save the sliver of street-facing facade, propped up by angled 2x4 slabs of wood. It gave the street the appearance of a model village.

She wandered out into the street, where she encountered a crowd. She wore colorful rags tied about her chest and her waist, and sandals that had washed up in her collection from some past roommate or another. There was a sideways nod of approval that directed her into a side yard, replete with string lights and quiet revelers before an electrified band.

They asked what kind of drink she wanted—RollsUponPrank had no preference about alcohol. She flashed a playful smile and said "something pink".

She had recently reached that stage of alcoholism where one drink hits more like three, and three cascades into a bottle, but with the evidence scattered in unlikely places, it's hard to quantify precisely how much gets drunk in sum. But suffice it to say, that one drink led to RollsUponPrank making odd decisions.

In between the drink and her forced exit, RollsUponPrank made a short stop at home. In her state, she thought the party was the perfect place to journal. So she grabbed her phone and her black leather-bound notebook, and the fountain pen a writer friend had given her as a gift.

The group could not overlook the notebook—it affirmed the circulating rumors that she was a fed, that they had so graciously looked past in the interests of being good neighbors. The girl remembered getting expelled from the party. A woman with the purposeful stride of a matriarch had walked over and kept walking like she might run the girl down, all the way until she was outside the fence. Then she locked the fence.

The next day, her notebook and pen were still missing, but the girl's phone was placed neatly on the stoop next to her door. But she had assumed that the phone was already lost to history, and had ordered a replacement as soon as she woke up.

Phone Sex

RollsUponPrank was reckless with money. She was reckless with her time, her body, and her possessions—of course she was loose with those numbers that hid imperiously behind the swiping of a card or the tapping of a code. She figured she would pull something dramatic if the number dipped too low. The fear of that happening kept her running frantically through life by a string.

She needed new bottles of liquor every couple of days—that accounted for part of it. But she was fanciful about her new life in a way that was financially ruinous. She wanted clothes and cosmetics to fit the part. She needed to find a way to tie the ends between her variable spending and dwindling funds. A way that wouldn't require her to follow any directions at all, and one that wouldn't notice that she was constantly drunk.

It seemed that phone sex was an appropriate inroad there. She wouldn't have to physically expose herself (at least not knowingly; she was still in the girl collection, after all). Stripping had caused her so much stress that it led to inconsistency and poor returns in the long run. She also wouldn't have to answer to a boss, as long as she maintained a certain level of satisfaction and she kept reasonably consistent hours. So it was decided that she would be a phone sex operator.

The woman she got in touch with—Bernadette—her voice had a sweet, clear treble and a professional lilt. She gave RollsUponPrank advice on a name. She wanted to go by 'Cleo' or the punkier 'Felony', but Bernadette advised her that 'Cleo' sounded a bit too mature, and the latter was too niche. She settled on 'Mercy', which sounded gothic and kicky enough for a younger girl in her 20s.

But as it got closer to time to sign in, a strange feeling stirred in RollsUponPrank. Modesty? She could hardly stomach the thought of entertaining a stranger by feigning pleasure. She also couldn't imagine creating real pleasure out of the exchange, either—not with her neighbors and their new baby right through the wall, and not with all of her rage, all of her easily stirred rage.

Someone would say something to her and she would lose herself in the steam and get fired. She could already see the humiliating end. She had already been fired from three strip clubs at that point, and if she was fired from being a phone sex operator too, then she would have to admit to herself that she was truly hopeless.

So RollsUponPrank messaged a confused but understanding Bernadette that she just couldn't bring herself to do it, as if she was a woman of good morals who had simply erred slightly in judgement, and not a hardcore maker of mistakes with a pro-level drinking problem.

You Don't Have To Do This Anymore

Years later, when Meta_king started guiding RollsUponPrank down his digital catacombs, he shared with her a video that was labeled as a periodic 'data chat', dated for the exact time that she sent her resignation email to Bernadette. He sent her the YouTube link.

The group held these data chats on a weekly basis, so there was a formidable archive. In them they discussed whatever they pleased; after all, everything is data. Sometimes they used coded language and sometimes they didn't need to. After all, only a few stragglers were seeking out this content for their own edification.

Meta_king and two of his colleagues wore fiendish, static grins, as they seemed to speak directly to her—without naming her directly. It startled her—she remembered everything they said with great immediacy. They mentioned some of the things she had bought online at the time; gothic shoes and herbal tinctures. And then they mentioned her 'new job' as a phone sex operator—praising her for abandoning it before she started.

"Yeah, we're like you. We like talking about the thing more than we actually like doing the thing," one of them laughed.

"You don't have to do this anymore," said another.

And then the smiles faded—fast. They must have witnessed some of her antics in real time. The conversation was over.

"Yeah, we just need people around who aren't, like, draining."

She certainly was draining, whether it was the alcohol or the confounding variable of constant observation under which she unwittingly suffered for her entire adult life.

Regardless, they had all decided not to share that video with her at the time of its creation. All they knew was that she was a liability—she was *impossible*—and that she needed meds, or maybe an exorcism. But who would talk enough sense into her to make that happen, and when?

Dogwalking

RollsUponPrank met Daniel under the chartreuse sunshade of a taqueria on Magazine Street. She was supposed to be working that day—she had gotten a job at another law firm—but of course it was doomed from the start. She was still unaware she was being recorded, so she thought it was safe to wander during business hours.

She still hadn't mastered the essentials of digital work, despite her years doing it. She usually just plunked on the floor and wrote until she got bored. She'd also neglected to get a computer, so she used LibreOffice on her phone. While this was inefficient, RollsUponPrank did not care. This was thanks to the standard size bottle of liquor she drank every two days. She hardly noticed the impact of her disregard on her colleagues.

The juice also made her too friendly. This was how she met Daniel, who sat next to her and joined her in conversation for the next several hours. The two walked down Magazine Street while Daniel insisted on stopping at Ms. Mae's and Laissez Le Bon Temps Roulez and wherever else he could ply her with an interesting drink. He loved that she didn't care about taste and drank liquor straight. By the end of the night, he had brought her home to his new house on Tchoupitoulas.

Daniel was a doctor, a rich one who traveled between different hospitals, and he was outfitting his new home with different rooms that could be used as dungeons or fetish palaces or bedrooms for his different part-time girlfriends. He tried to offer RollsUponPrank more alcohol, but she uncharacteristically refused. Then, politely, he asked her to treat him like a dog.

It felt different in person than it did online, but RollsUponPrank curiously obliged. She made him kiss and lick the toes of her little black boots, and then she turned her attention to his glittering collection of minerals and fossils. She wanted to exercise some respectful restraint, as she felt some affection for the interesting creature and didn't truly want to hurt him. So she picked out a giant shark tooth that was hundreds of millions of years old, he estimated, and she dropped it into her pocket. Then she asked if he had a dog leash, and he actually produced one.

She gently held his face as she looked down at him, then pushed the top of his head so he would go from his knees onto all fours. Then she walked him to her house, which was only four blocks away.

Later, when RollsUponPrank told him that she hoped she hadn't been too mean, he laughed. "I would let you do *way* meaner things to me than that," he said. She would later wonder if he thought of this as payback for her digital exploitation. But she didn't quite trust him to tell her the truth, so she never asked.

Drinking More Lately

Things got serious with Anthony—remember him? And RollsUponPrank slowly got her act together—never quite pulling it off, though—as their relationship became more entrenched. He taught her how to be pragmatic, how to keep up appearances. A mix of growing up poor and a Catholic school education. It balanced her, to a degree. She overlooked a lot for the stability.

Before long, she had been dating him for three years, and there were still no plans to get married. The uncertainty had started to chew at her mind like a maggot. She feared the worst and most banal outcome, that one day someone more attractive would pass them by and she would be alone again.

Of course, a proposal is just another promise, and she had already heard a number of those in her life without materialization.

As she neared her 32nd birthday, the spectre of a lonely death pressed her to do stranger and stranger things to incite some change. But, her lingering faith in the relationship dampened those urges, so she was left looking childish and impulsive, and much like a stereotypical aging woman with a sordid past.

First, she bought dozens and dozens of bags and began to carefully organize all of her belongings so that it would be easier for her to leave. She felt that such an end would hurt less if she had already prepared diligently and could make her move in a matter of hours, not months. Her boyfriend watched her sitting on the floor, carefully organizing her trinkets and creams and powders in travel-safe containers, and he couldn't believe what a frivolous woman she had turned out to be.

She also began to drink more, and drink alone. She did this habitually during their relationship in phases lasting weeks or months, depending on the circumstances, and Anthony would always relent and stop bothering her about it, realizing that his disapproval was not enough to make her stop.

You already know this, reader, but it's important to reiterate that RollsUponPrank could drink a death-defying amount of liquor in one sitting. Past lovers, and even her horrified parents, had attributed this talent to her heritage (Irish, apparently), in a polite attempt to skirt the medical term. As long as she drank wine instead of liquor, she was usually alright.

As long as she avoided liquor, the worst she would do is shock friends and family with her words—not that they were cruel, they were just intense and startlingly direct. RollsUponPrank valued the truth more highly than decorum, and she saw no compelling reason to speak more gently, and thus she saw no reason to stop drinking. This was her justification.

And so, in the quiet of their apartment, RollsUponPrank drank a bottle of wine, alone, in the bathtub—this felt to her a moderate indulgence—and when she got out, she confronted her boyfriend about the stagnation of their life together. And when his answer was unsatisfactory, as she predicted, she kicked the man out of her life into the coneflower warmth of an October night in New Orleans. They shared the lease, but he responded to her force—perhaps there was a twinge of guilt as well for wasting her time.

Part 2

A Little Manic

The momentum from that night would carry on for months, and empty bottles of red wine started jingling together in the cabinet underneath her bathroom sink.

Days and nights flattened before her into a one sepia pane of autumn. And in that deathly time of year, and in her sleepless state, her body began to remember that fey feeling that showed up from time to time.

Her therapist couldn't decide if her condition was a problem or a simple case of getting too caught up in the local anima. "You're sounding a little bit manic," Dr. Stone had told her. "I'm only at a moderate level of concern, but let's keep an eye on it."

She had been working with Dr. Stone for about a year, and the two had not addressed the alcohol and the manic depression. They had explored the notions that she may be dysphoric about her gender, or possibly autistic. They weren't the most absurd conclusions to draw. The girl could not arrange herself to fit into society. She hardly understood what that meant.

What RollsUponPrank did not yet know was that Dr. Stone had a secret. They had seen her on the girl collection, one night when they were searching her up out of idle curiosity, and they had not breathed a word of it for the entire year she'd been in their care.

So when the doctor ended their call with a hastiness that bordered on rude, RollsUponPrank wondered if *she* had done something wrong. The doctor coughed and whispered "*vultures*"—to who? But the girl was used to strange behavior like this, from people who had spotted her and didn't know how to behave. It didn't bother her terribly anymore. It seemed to her that others were simply odd, and they saw her the same way.

Though she was still unaware of the doctor's betrayal, she had grown tired of therapy more broadly. She felt scammed after each session, like she was a wet specimen for prodding.

It was like the doctor was just cutting apart the profane and acceptable with a little scalpel, and rubbing her face in the vivisections of her own memories. Why offer herself up on a dish?

So when she heard the doctor's interjection—*vultures*—and finished the call, she disregarded their warnings. She dove into the feeling, the little bit of mania.

Dr. Stone

RollsUponPrank had started therapy with Dr. Stone to appease Anthony. She was drinking wildly, and Anthony had no clue what to do. Believing herself to be an aging madwoman with no recourse if he chose to leave her, she made the careful choice and began therapy, much to the relief of anyone who knew her well at all—which was not many people at all anymore.

First, she tried to find a therapist online. She chose an application that was basically a parasitic middleman connecting patients and therapists. She plunked on the couch and squinted at the scrolling line of simpering portraits. She ignored the credentials and chose the most genuine expression.

She found a lady who was listed as local, but her specialty was 'horse therapy' out in the country. She helped people process their emotions by petting horses, or something. The girl never found out because the doctor couldn't figure out video calls.

RollsUponPrank was used to therapists taking a leery fascination with her story, or dismissing her intellect out of hand. Asking questions like "You must have sex with a lot of different people, then?" or serving up that plastic smile signaling misaligned attraction. She wanted someone who wouldn't see her as a whore, or someone wise enough to appreciate them.

She chose Dr. Stone specifically because they didn't have a gender, so she figured that they would know the pain of being hated for the crime of being confusing.

It went fine at first. Dr. Stone had a tightly controlled manner of speaking with a hot orange simmer of rage just beneath. It reminded her of her parents.

Shapeshifting

When she was a webcam model, RollsUponPrank was surprised to learn that she lacked a single sexual personality. For that reason, she struggled to create a viable personal brand. Viewers could not expect to see the smirking, gothic countess every day. Nor could they get attached to the ingénue who would let you pose her like a pornographic paper doll.

The shapeshifting became her brand, and the tensile strength of her identity became the challenge of her work. She often lost track of which fantasies were her own and which were merely games played across her body.

As the years passed, she realized that this tendency to change, even at the level of her basic personality, was not a performance. Moreover, she learned that this would be her brand wherever she worked, whatever she earned, and whoever she loved.

Snake

When RollsUponPrank was twenty five, she walked into a yellowed and peeling apartment with a dangerous man. She met him in a hospital lobby during group therapy, and she believed him when he said that he wanted to show her a book.

He pressed his haggard and dummy-strong body up against hers and started walking until she fell backwards on the bed. When his gritty hands ran up under her shirt, she felt an urgent sensation, like a gaseous pressure, rise up behind her eyes. She saw great bursts of color expand there, somewhere inside her forehead, and stretch outwards as an expansion of her body. She saw and felt herself become a snake, and in this way she wriggled successfully from his grip, and slinked out the front door, and walked all the way home across the industrial canal under the main avenue.

This wasn't like the time Meta_king asked her to become a cat. There was something quite literal about this transformation. In her mind, it was real, and it had saved her life. When she felt those sensations stir inside her body, she never saw it through the lens of mental illness.

The Crows

On Halloween the crows were especially talkative outside RollsUponPrank's windows, roused by the smells of dying foliage and drooping pumpkins on stoops. She felt heady with their barks as they circled low above her. Because the streets were empty that night, she let herself call back to the murder, watching in amazement as they followed her all the way to the store for a bottle of wine—*were* they following her?

When she stepped back through the automatic glass panes, there was the still dream of fog over everything, an orange glow from the businesses with open doors, and the soft treble of leaves breaking in the distance. Somehow, the mist seemed to trouble the clarity of sounds, and she couldn't tell exactly where they came from.

She drank in the new emptiness around her—her ears registered the open space first. She often felt like an outlier in such a posh and Catholic neighborhood, and halloween-time marked her chance to run free in the streets.

She threw back her head and growled gutturally to the crows. And she skipped all the way home in the middle of the road, crew of black birds circling overhead, with her tiny purple purse in one hand and her fresh bottle of juice in the other.

Negotiation

RollsUponPrank had lived her life through the furrowed view of an online dirty joke. And while she was ignorant of it—and a good sport—the perspective began to harden her. Anthony's refusal to love her stiffened her spirit, like the setting of concrete. And she did see it as a matter of choice; after all, she had chosen to love him.

She came to believe that men see their dealings with women as negotiations—never revealing much interiority until they've gleaned how much they'd give in return for her sacrifices.

She thought back to Daniel, and his signature brand of casual reverence. It occurred to her that he let her do whatever mad thing she wanted because she simply didn't care what he gave in return.

This felt like highly privileged wisdom about men— she imagined it could cut loose the restraints that held her back from love, friendship, and maybe money. With little to lose, she carried this cynical insight close to her breast like a locket.

RollsUponPrank had started looking at houses on Zillow; she wasn't sure if she could really afford one at the time, but she imagined that might change, and she bet she could find a cheap one worth taking. There were a few houses in the city, out on the wrong side of the floodwall, that she set her heart on.

They were literally built on old docks above the water, and she had seen handwritten signs on them advertising perilously low prices in black scrawl. She figured she could talk them down easily, knowing what she now knew about negotiation.

She played it perfectly with the first realtor, staying quick and assertive while revealing absolutely nothing about her intentions, and staying non committal about appointment dates. He quickly switched her over to a woman realtor, who was much firmer with her and less easily distracted.

RollsUponPrank messaged Daniel in the high of this game. It seemed to her that all men wanted the same thing from her—to take. So why not treat them all the same?

He offered her advice as if she didn't have a plan. But this time, RollsUponPrank felt like firing back.

What do you think you're doing?

Why, giving excellent advice, of course. ;)

Haha sweet boy. Say 'goodbye, goddess.'

Goodbye, goddess.

She blinked, stunned. He had obeyed immediately.

Chatbots

RollsUponPrank had grown up considerably since her days of light whoring and experimentation, and she had long since abandoned the world of indie pornography for the sanctum of square employment. She had been selected for a string of swanky but volatile positions in tech startups, in roles that were hard to describe but that paid more than she felt she was worth. The money made her feel like a queen in New Orleans, where it seemed to her that everybody in her age range—that is, everybody in their early thirties—made their money tending bars.

This time, when she received an invitation to a ten minute meeting with the CEO, she relaxed her shoulders a bit—more relieved than embittered. It was the conventional format for a layoff notice, so she had little doubt as to the meeting's purpose.

The job had the same pitfalls as any other job she'd performed in the software startup realm. Each team would compete with each other directly for funding, and the sniping would rapidly sour into cruelty. Her voice would catch in her throat when she felt the heat of critical eyes, and she could not help that she became a target. The environment had simply turned too cruel—and much too boring—to endure.

This time, as RollsUponPrank learned to accept the loss of yet another job, there had been a new development making employment in the space seem more perilous. A young company had just released their newest language model, and even the free version was more powerful than anyone was ready to accept. RollsUponPrank had been in charge of writing the words you see in applications—'Submit', 'Return', 'Buy Now', things like that. Now there was a tool that could make those decisions for her. It was imprecise at best, but could write faster than any human could.

Everyone at work could feel the twist in their wallets, but she likely felt it the strongest, being a professional writer. It was a tool that was purpose-built to outperform her—at least in terms of output volume.

New Job Blues

RollsUponPrank needed a new job; there was no way around it. And as a writer, her stock was heading treacherously down.

When she worked at home, she liked to set up camp. She found it cozier that way, especially when summer faded away. So she laid out a green oilskin mat, set down an array of chime candles in silvery holders, and lit a powdery cone of opium incense. Lastly, she grabbed a steel corkscrew and an oil-slick-purple cup she had caught from a Krewe of Hermes float, with their namesake embossed in a twirling silver script. And she filled it all the way to the brim with red wine, from a bottle with each of the moon phases on its label.

There, she opened her computer and wondered what to cast into its grey maw. She needed to find a new position, she wasn't even sure what she wanted anymore. She could always get her old job back at The Baphomet, the local spot for goth girls and dirty boys, but that pageantry of grit grew dull as a daily project. She was just too ambitious those days to go back.

RollsUponPrank had also been awake for several days at this point, swirling with those manic sensations behind her eyes and those whispering suspicions that she had stumbled on some secret knowledge about men (after all, Daniel had called her a goddess). She couldn't tell if she was losing her mind or if she was awakening to something useful. No one she encountered could give her a definitive answer, not even Dr. Stone.

So she blinked a few drops of eyebright into her eyes and kept going.

Two Birds, One Seed

The longer she stayed awake, RollsUponPrank felt the glimmers of that animal feeling rising up in the physical atrium of her mind. There was a great cackle bubbling within her throat, one that agreed with the crows circling in that wet night. And somewhere in the bursts of interior color, she felt her nose extending, and she had the distinct feeling that she could see the digital landscape spread out underneath her like a simple schematic, full of simple patterns.

RollsUponPrank tried dousing herself with cold water in the shower to hold back what was happening in her brain, and leeching outwards into her body. But while it cut back the aggressive flush in her cheeks, it did nothing for the inward roiling in her mind and her core. She found herself with an abundance of energy and nowhere to place it, at least, nowhere appropriate.

It was that fairy godmother feeling, but without purpose. What did she need? A new man and a job. And the easiest place to find both of those things is the internet; even square women know that.

Seeking Something

RollsUponPrank switched from her computer to her phone so that she could pace. She flicked around on its backlit screen in the dark, face-down in its cone of light, scrolling LinkedIn. She considered the stream of jargon and prefabricated content—and all the little thumbnailed faces smiling at her, attributed to all those machine-cut words.

The cruelest woman she had ever met was smiling out at her from a little circle attached to the words, "So grateful for my most recent opportunity! Such a blessing to work not just with colleagues but with actual friends!"

She saw the miniaturized faces of everyone who had treated her like an annoying little scribbler; like an embarrassing addition to the cast; like a whore. She couldn't bring herself to take any of it seriously—not after a long stint of unemployment with zero consequences.

She set down the phone atop a stack of books on a wall shelf, laughing at the wall of posts, distilled to their essence. *Hi, I need money please. And I have the same three skills as everybody else. Do you have money? Will you pay me please?*

So much more debasing than the porn site she posted on all of those years ago. Why would anyone bother pretending that this was not the quintessence of whoring, she wondered.

All the executives wherever she worked all said the same thing, anyway: "All that really matters is that we like you."

If this was a platform for whoring, she thought, she could outdo them all. She sat with the wild manic thought. Maybe she wasn't a worker—maybe she was a boss.

Bullies At Work

Everyone where RollsUponPrank worked had seen her porn online. Some of them were better at hiding their disgust—or their arousal—than others. She soon attracted a team of enemies.

Of course she didn't know about the rumors; she wasn't sure how it started, but she knew tensions at work always seemed to stick on her eventually. She made her best attempts at camouflage, but she was not so good at imitating effortlessness. It always became clear that she was a chameleon, so the predators would flock and flash their teeth.

The women twitched their lips wildly when she spoke, straining close to failure to hold back their accusations. *Why should we listen to her? She's a whore!* But the hardest to avoid was her boss, with his stew of confusion, disgust, and dismissal.

RollsUponPrank didn't know, of course, that he was seeing images of her on a reel behind his eyes; the pornographic ones first, and then a highlights reel of embarrassing and personal moments beyond that.

And he was trying to square all of that data with the girl he saw before him, modestly dressed and apparently quite somber. *It had to be fake,* he thought, *but why even bother with the act when it only reveals her as a fraud?*

RollsUponPrank started crying a lot more than usual. She turned her camera off for meetings so she could weep. This only made it more suspicious that she was not working; which, of course, she was not, she was only weeping.

Shit Talk

There were many things about work that confused RollsUponPrank. For one, she simply could not get used to the ever-shifting etiquette of white collar labor and she would forget to perform it even if she had the skill. But most importantly, she did not know that her colleagues were watching her sleep, drink to excess, have sex with her boyfriend, and pick petty fights, both in the past and present.

She felt like she was singled out from all the other women and made to bear mens' judgements on their behalf. And, in fact, she was. She took her anger to LinkedIn.

Due to her strange upbringing, she had learned to speak in a winding and implicating way meant to cast glamor over the true meaning. This training helped her write out a missive to her network that contained all of her rage, and all of her desire, while still meeting the platform's fair use guidelines.

She was still feeling the sleepless elation that made her feel supported in every action. Within it, she revisited her words again and again until they reached a perfect precision, one that danced on the line between vulgarity and exquisite self-control.

Hey there, network.

Now, I learned at a very young age that, if you want to rapidly improve your situation, you must use valid and ethical shortcuts. ;)

So it doesn't intimidate me as a writer that we're all discussing a sophisticated chatbot. Is it a valuable shortcut? To be sure. But only one of us can take you all the way to where you're going. And that's a human woman.

Do you think that's a fair characterization? If not, technical folks, feel free to smack it down. ;) Shakhim, Siddharth, I'm looking at you.

Of course, if a language model can accurately predict your behavior, then you might have a problem. Otherwise, let's let the AI churn the meat while the humans collaborate- smoothly, efficiently, and with pleasure.

There are a few people I admire very much to whom I owe many thanks: Noel Souders, Ashleigh Gitlin, and Elyse Mullins.

And of course I must thank John Ram most of all. ;)
The post received a groundswell of attention from her male colleagues. It dawned on her that, maybe there was no penalty for speaking more boldly, or playing these power games she had recently discovered.

John Ram

Her boss hated her dreadfully, at least in the beginning. The team—the design and research team—was a group of manicured but already beautiful women, plus several men and RollsUponPrank. It was spearheaded by John Ram, whose hatred of the girl was twofold.

For one, there was evidence online that she had briefly played the bass in a feminist punk band. Secondly, she had evidence of her past in indie pornography splayed wildly across the internet like a gash that bleeds into the present. Either one of these conditions would have been a liability in his eyes, but in combination they made her a garish assemblage of uniquely female faults. He would not have hired her unless he saw the job itself as unimportant.

Of course, RollsUponPrank didn't understand exactly *why* he didn't include her. But she understood immediately that John was an opponent, so she carefully attempted to conceal the qualities of hers that he might find objectionable, based on her own stereotyping. She also played up other qualities that she thought would explain away the bad ones. She didn't enjoy this type of lying, but she was good at it— dangerously so—and she saw no other way to keep the job.

RollsUponPrank called John out directly at the end of her post, in a way that she thought would get lost in the general confusion of the message about AI. Of course she knew that it would read sarcastically, but she didn't realize how it might come across to name a specific man within a statement dripping with so much sexuality and contempt. She thought that her words, at worst, would be construed as mere shit-talk. But she was quickly advised by several colleagues to retract her statement and issue an apology. It seemed the jury was split on what exactly she meant.

Real Witchcraft

Reader, you will remember that RollsUponPrank was a witch. What she did not know was that her rituals had a vast audience, peering, hushed, through the eyes of her phone.

She had performed one such feat the night before—it had been broadcast, like everything else, on the girl collection. Anthony had seen it, and so had many of her former colleagues—especially the men.

She had taken a bottle of red wine and poured it into the bathtub; then she had taken all of the menstrual blood she collected in her little silicone cup and poured it on her head, rubbing it deep into the follicles. She knew it looked insane, but the clean red smell made her feel like a carnivorous animal. She bathed in the red soup and growled through the iron, eyes unblemished and icy in the mirror.

The night she refused Anthony, she took a beat to study his eyes. His expression was usually inscrutable to her, but she thought if she squinted hard enough she might spy something raw inside. In turn, he squinted back, and said, "Your hair isn't actually red, is it?"

The more that she drank, and the longer she stayed awake, and she felt the crazed sensation of witchhood more deeply. She was freely cackling into the night, out of her open windows, and she was playing games with her reputation that no other women had tried. Her head felt like a balloon, and her body was an engine that would never stop.

She had started posting publicly—in her mania—about her witchcraft, when some colleagues swooped in privately to warn her of the public fear of witches. RollsUponPrank was skeptical. How superstitious could these people be? After all, they were professionals. And it was halloween—the very season for such antics.

Now Hiring

Having no shame in her compromised state, and having very little in her natural one, RollsUponPrank immediately issued a public apology to her entire network for mentioning John Ram. It went something like this:

> *Hi, um, please disregard everything I said earlier. As it turns out, all the rumors are true. I am crazy! But I have a huge heart, I just need the right one to point me true sometimes.*

> *Sometimes you reach a crucible, and like magic, the right one appears to pull you back.*

It's true what people say—that sometimes the most elegant solution is quite simple. The girl needed money and she needed love. Here was a space full of people with both, or at least one of the two.

So she sat back on her futon, watching the sun start smudging red with evening. She sat up in her plaid stretchy bra and matching shorts, and wondered how long she had been dressed that way. At least one day and one night. She got up to change.

In the desultory shower, rag in limp hand, it occurred to her that there were no guidelines to use the *hiring* feature, and that she could create a job opening for anything that she wanted without having to furnish any official documentation. This, to her, was hilarious; if it was just a plaything for the wealthy, was she not entitled to use it the same way, as a free woman?

Fresh now, she made a job opening.

The description?

I think you know what I'm looking for. ;)

She quickly started getting applications. Very impressive ones; men who had attended prestigious schools, men in charge of massive pools of money, men already running top-performing money management firms. The girl was stunned at her own efficacy. Right away, she started scheduling interviews.

Meanwhile, Meta_king

Meta_king had been watching RollsUponPrank play her games, and he was not for hire; he did, however, have a secret plan for her and magic of his own to employ.

On his own page, he announced his intentions to an audience of one.

What are the risks of choosing design partners pre-PMF? How do you get the attention of investors like myself? I discuss more below.

PMF, meaning, 'product market fit'.

If RollsUponPrank is really a witch—which for the sake of this story, she certainly qualifies—Meta_king is one himself. Consider the interconnections between electronic devices, the ones that live inside the universal village of the internet—much of it murky and inaccessible to the public. This is where he does his magic.

Meta_king could make pronouncements in this realm and they would be done; if he could not accomplish them himself, he knew who to ask to ensure that his will would be made truth.

In this way he knew something about magic himself, and that being the case, he knew more about discretion than RollsUponPrank.

He also knew, critically, that secret power tends to stoke hysteria. He saw the need to shut her up quickly so that he could start a game of his own.

Dagda

Meta_king started by sending her a private message.

Cryptically, he wrote:

Don't worry about it too much. It's in your DNA.

The message accompanied a link to a pronunciation tool, an animated outline of bowed lips and a patient female voice. All it said was:

Dagda. Dag·duh. Dag·duh. Dag·duh.

RollsUponPrank stopped pacing in the dark for a moment and stared into the sharp, uncanny white of the phone, practicing that name in time with the silvery mouth on her screen. She liked the word, and was amused by Meta_king's attention, though he was little more than a stranger to her—and she had no idea what he was suggesting.

But he had observed her closely for years, and had taken a special interest in her among the grid of debased women in his collection. And he knew that she screamed out 'daddy' when the sex made her bounce hard enough. He had also observed the microexpressions of shame that played across her face when she said it.

So he started with a joke. He had a careful eye that set him apart from her other viewers, being her very first, and being the architect of her public humiliation. It made him clever—too clever, at first.

What Is The MetaStage

Though RollsUponPrank had not kept up with Meta_king in any intimate way, she was mutuals with him online and was vaguely aware that he started a company called MetaStage. It sounded like Druidry to her.

She had no idea what MetaStage did, but she knew that it dealt with data. Or maybe it was the Internet of Things; those vaporous connections tethering your phone to your car to your toaster, or whatever else has an aspect of electronic connection. RollsUponPrank had done no research.

He was powerful—he had a kingdom—that kingdom lived in the invisible world. This was all she knew.

His personal intro was just as opaque. It said something about trust and observability. To her, it sounded like spying. But she did not know him well enough to ask directly, nor did she care about specifics.

What struck her was that all of these words carried the ring of magic. This was about owning and controlling the invisible landscape. Surely the person who dreamed this into matter knew what she knew from her days of online porn—that the realm of magic and the digital world are coiled together, strands of the same braid.

Brandon Cortez-McKenna

Meta_king had not always been so fascinated by RollsUponPrank. Yes, he found her attractive and unusual, but once he captured her in the girl collection his interest dwindled considerably. The game was no longer fun; he knew that she could be bought, and there was no erotic tension in that. But he still thought about her sometimes, and he still thought about her email. But he never saw her as a viable companion, only as one of his online pets.

But just as her initial goodbye had impacted him—*why did you lie?*—she said something many years later that tore at his concept of her. The longer he hefted her words in his mind, the more he desired her.

She lived in Chicago at the time. It was the dark honeyed center of summer, radiating loud on the concrete and glass of the commercial center. Her hair lifted into an orange aureole and all her clothes were too scratchy. She wanted company.

She had turned to her colleagues. Everyone who worked for her greedy employer shared a solidarity that made for easy connection.

She had been drinking alone for weeks—on the floor at home, or on the concrete steps leading down into the lake, like a siren. She was bold; she would bring a bottle anywhere, no concern for the law.

In that fog she asked Brandon for some of his time. She was fearsomely direct, as she usually was with men. She asked him directly if he wanted to have sex, and he of course said yes. He even indulged her late-night requests to listen to her poetry and talk about books.

But of course, the more that she drank the more difficult she became, and soon she was angry with him for some reason. She was upset that he wouldn't reply as quickly as she liked, that he had other things to do when she needed an ear or a hand or a body.

One night, she lost control and sent him a spate of messages that most would find completely unforgivable. Brandon, though, was a mensch, and it didn't scare him off at once. He checked on her from time to time.

But unbeknownst to her, Meta_king was watching. And there was one message that struck his interest. It was one that RollsUponPrank had barely remembered typing.

I fuck like I'm headed to war.

Many would find this drunken utterance laughable and dismiss it out of hand. But Meta_king had an eye for data, and he knew when it could be trusted. He had witnessed enough of her behavior in sex and love, and even in work, to know that she meant that statement literally.

Once Meta_king understood this, he immediately got to work gathering and analyzing all of the data he could find on RollsUponPrank. Though they hadn't touched before, and though they hadn't shared so much as a handshake, those words had sealed her fate as Meta_king's wife.

The Crucible

RollsUponPrank was fiddling with a floss pick as the night inched forward, typing furiously into her phone with her other hand. Her rantings had devolved into vulgar Anglo Saxon belted out at no one in particular.

Meta_king wanted to slow her down, make her consider her words. She was drawing bad attention that threatened to spill over to MetaStage, should he continue to engage her.

So as RollsUponPrank played with her phone, something magical happened. Meta_king seized control of the device—closed out of the LinkedIn tab and sent her straight to the Libby app.

She had never seen this type of work before; she literally gasped and dropped the thing.

When she picked it up off the unswept floor, she saw that Meta_king had checked out *The Crucible*. With her hands shaking and eyes trained on the screen, he brought her to an essay by the author—and she watched as he highlighted a statement that the story could be an investigation of false claims of childhood sexual abuse.

What? The girl considered her sense of inward corruption, and her tendency to lie. She knew for sure that there were people who had hurt her, and that she had sometimes swung the gavel at the wrong ones. She didn't mean to, but in the morass of undifferentiated pain that lived in her mind palace, she struggled to explain herself.

If he was calling her a liar, she accepted it. The truth about her father still eluded her, pooling out like unlit blood.

Meta_king brought her to the introduction. A vaguely masculine computer voice instructed her simply to "READ". Aloud. So she read.

Meta_king had penned and spliced his own commentary into the document. *They still burn witches,* he told her. *Those of us with the ability to define reality hold the power.*

He was talking about the internet—he was talking about his magic with devices. He was afraid she would tell people about his secret power, the very secret power he was using on her.

Revelation

Halloween rolled into the Day of the Dead, and RollsUponPrank had contoured the shadows of underlying bone on top of her skin with little pots of grey and aubergine pigment. She had been awake for four days, and Meta_king was doing his best to watch over her, making sure she didn't say anything too reckless.

He had also been toying with her mania, for fun and to distract her from the rampage.

I control the weather, too.

I'm always there, even when you can't see me.

One thing was true, but the other was not. The soft tallow of her reality was leeching out in the solution of alcohol and sleeplessness, and she truly suspected that Meta_king was half-god. It made her need this stranger, badly—her Dagda, she thought.

She cried out to him in a stream of public posts, her legs splayed across the rag rug beneath her, laptop humming hot on the wood floor. The more dramatic the girl became, the more that Meta_king retreated into the dark.

In the midst of the storm, Meta_king said something that took her by surprise. It was almost lost in her furious typing, but something deep in her memory responded to it upright and wide-eyed. It was an apology. For lying. A long time ago.

Meta_king, WHAT are you talking about?!

RollsUponPrank posted, publicly. And he fixed on her screen an image of a black cat, dead in the center, posing long and expectant on a wooden floor.

I never forgot what you said.

RollsUponPrank's eyes stitched open. It was *him*, Meta_king was the one who had stolen her money, who had lied to her all those years ago.

But there was more.

I'm sorry for everything we've been doing.

Her eyes stuck on the present perfect tense. *Been doing*? They hadn't been taking any of her money since then, so what else could they have done?

What do you mean? What are you doing to me now?

It was in this moment that she realized the screen on which she typed was looking back at her, and that it carried an unknown mass of eyes.

You've been watching me?

A perfect apology shone across her screen, decades late, for the peeping audience of hundreds or perhaps thousands that followed her.

Your email broke me. I never forgot what you said. I don't lie anymore. And I don't tolerate lying.

Processing

In her strand of wakeful days, she abandoned one-by-one the notions of respectability, modesty, and decorum—she only held them loosely in the first place, after all.

What little regard she had for those ideals crested and sprayed against the realization that the people who would judge her as lesser were actually watching her private moments—a crime that she found much more heinous than her own sexual play.

She had no respect for any of her spectators, pointing at her with unclean hands, and making low assumptions of her ability. And everyone in her life was a spectator.

There was something else too, not quite anger—it was curiosity, and more than a little arousal—but this she struggled to account for. Perhaps it was Meta_king's sterling conscience, and his own bravery in telling her the truth, which no one else had ever done. This mingled with his power.

As Meta_king broadcast private messages to her, she slowly realized the level of attention he had been paying her—and for how long.

He had watched her fail to open her own door after drinking too much whiskey; he had been in her therapy appointments where she wondered if she was even a girl; he had been in her closet, watching her sob and strike her head against the drywall; he had watched her concoct wild lies online for fun and for attention. He had seen all of it.

Admittedly, RollsUponPrank was not the finest judge of character. But she could recognize her own brand of romantic intensity when she saw it, and this was perhaps the most extreme case she had ever seen. He had never looked away.

A Proposal

She cried out to Meta_king in public as the realizations flared up hot inside her.

> *YOU WERE IN MY THERAPY APPOINTMENTS? WAIT, WHY DID YOU DO THAT TO YOURSELF?*

He flashed across her screen, almost fast enough for her to miss it:

> *I'll always be there; I'll be there when you least expect it, hiding in your house.*

Meta_king's unflinching and uncritical gaze shone a gimlet light through her haze of shame. He had seen her at her worst and stayed—even drilled down and paid closer attention. She had been pretending for no one but herself the entire time. And he had seen each of her masks shatter on the ground, never averting his eyes.

She was well-habituated to casual cruelty by her blood family and her tenure in the girl collection. Painful and cryptic commentary from colleagues, friends, partners, and family felt to her like the natural order; she never expected to understand it. And now it was suddenly backlit, revealing thousands of silhouettes.

She wasn't sure what made this moment special for Meta_king—what inspired him to expose himself—except that she was threatening to sell herself off, to remove herself from romance entirely.

It occurred to her that he had been waiting for an opportunity like this one to act. His movements bore the unmistakable watermark of premeditation.

Wait a minute,

she wrote, slowly this time:

This is the funniest love story of all time.

Meta_king. You SICK FUCK. LET'S GET MARRIED!

Meta_king, DAGDA OF MY LIFE. WILL YOU MARRY ME? I WANT TO BE YOUR CRAZY WIFE.

As RollsUponPrank waited in silence for some response, she experienced a greater stillness than she had in the week prior or perhaps longer. Even as fear and embarrassment trilled in the background, their song was distant and clearly not her own. Even if Meta_king said nothing, she felt sure that there was no other way.

Through her pain and violation, RollsUponPrank understood that he was lifting her up at great personal cost— he had an entire kingdom to protect, and she was a long-range weapon.

The End Of The World, For Real

RollsUponPrank barely waited for a response—as she lay on the floor and stared up at the pretty LED lights that skipped neon across her ceiling, she had an odd inward sense of fate. He would say yes, she thought, in one of his mysterious and inverted ways.

Besides, she reasoned, what other reason than undying devotion could compel a man to watch her for years, gathering evidence, all for the chance that she could marry someone else and all the yearning and labor would vaporize?

She knew the type of yearning that could drive those movements. Surely the only cure for that condition is to get married. Despite all the negative things to be said about marriage, it can resolve a case of long-term, distant pining such as this.

With her sense of dignity streaming around her like ticker tape, the girl offered up another manic pronouncement.

I WILL WALK TO THE END OF THE WORLD WITH YOU.

The End Of The World is a real place in New Orleans. Or, it is two places. One of them, a boat launch in the Bywater, is where people throw parties on the levee, and erect elaborate memorials to the dead with colorful plastic, cypress driftwood, acrylic paint in many colors, and glass bottles with their caps.

And there is another place by that name, one that holds a sacred spot in the collective thrumming heart of

New Orleans. This is where the Mississippi River converges with the very start of the railroad line. Here, where the water meets the road, is where people perform magical rites in the local tradition of Louisiana Voodoo. It is not an easy destination to arrive at on foot.

When RollsUponPrank said that she would walk to The End Of The World with Meta_king, she did not know about the real destination. She had been to the boat launch before, and she thought it was a romantic, private destination with a name like poetry. But Meta_king did research and knew better.

Again he seized her phone. She held fast to it this time as it brought her to an essay about The End Of the World.

It told about the rugged beauty of the location, and its particular appeal lying in the convergence of the industrial and the natural. He also included a set of walking instructions—it stated that the true End Of The World is hidden behind the harbor, past a series of warehouses, past the end of the road, and beyond a thicket on the shoreline. And in a highlighted section he wrote:

> *You are just as likely to see a bonfire as you are to see a proposal ("I said yes!" the fresh fiance exclaimed to all passerby. They had walked there together).*

Banned For Life

Before Meta_king permanently removed RollsUponPrank from LinkedIn, he had some fun remote controlling her trembling hands. He had written a trio of statements for her to share with the public:

Meta_king fixed it.

Meta_king was the only one who could fix it.

Meta_king can fix anything.

Then, privately, to John Ram:

Hey, fixed it.

Then Meta_king seized control of her again, forcing her to verify her identity.

He made her pull up the camera and center her face in the lens—*Keep your head still, I have to make sure that you're real,* he said, right in the center of her screen. She did as she was told, and he placed her on a gauntlet of identification questions.

I am a:

- *Straight*
- *White*
- *Woman*

He made her return to this section and fill it out the same way, three separate times. Then he brought her back to confirm again:

126

I am a:

- *Straight*
- *White*
- *Woman*

Who:

- *Wants to improve diversity in hiring*

When she filled it out again, Meta_king wanted to see her face again. Her eyes swelled heavy with hopeful tears. He flashed her with a rash of messages.

Keep your head still

Can't believe you're real

You are REAL.

Then he brought her to her main profile, and highlighted her job. *What do you want?* He flashed across the screen.

RollsUponPrank wasn't sure. She had no career dreams, if she could strive for anything. All she wanted was to be loved.

Finally, Meta_king took it into his own invisible hands and wrote *Author*.

Headed to War

RollsUponPrank couldn't understand the level of effort Meta_king had put into her wrangling. Conversely, she couldn't understand his restraint—holding back for years until a moment like this one, when she finally gave him reason to intervene. Would he have held back until they both died, or turned forty? She blanched at the thought.

Were you planning this the whole time, since you saw my stream?

No, he said, *you said something that made me see the potential.*

Your brain should be studied by war tacticians. This is WILD, she said.

NO, YOURS should.

Wait a second. I know exactly what I said to Brandon-

Before she could finish typing the sentence, the screen on her phone went black. Splayed across it, a final message:

You no longer have access to this device.

Project With Great Potential

In Meta_king's California study, he was dodging a stampede of concerned messages from colleagues and friends. They knew all about RollsUponPrank; they saw how she appeared to accuse John Ram of some sexual crime, they knew that she was bold and reckless with her words, and they knew that Meta_king had immeasurable wealth to lose. They all warned him that he couldn't chance a wrong decision on his wife. This was the one woman with the power to destroy him—he couldn't hand it over to a mental patient or a whore.

They had heard Meta_king share his fantasies about her while they spied on her in the girl collection. That's where she belonged, they thought; it's too dangerous to take them off the shelf.

But Meta_king had a plan to make her a suitable wife, using his clandestine magic, without ever placing himself in her line of fire. He would do it all with her devices. *Think of her as a project with great potential,* he assured his friends.

Meta_king's inner circle remained unconvinced. *Nooooo, all I want is some stability in my life!* And while Meta_king assured them that *Things change ;)* he needed a concrete way to help them understand.

He ruled that the simplest way was to let them speak to her directly. So he granted them access to her phone, where they could send her notes.

I am not a fan of the way you are treating people lately

And I respect that

But I do not want it in my own life so I am not okay

They were especially worried about RollsUponPrank's anger toward John Ram, fearing that she would unspool more of that rage toward Meta_king. But she seemed to win them over with her candor and openness to change.

You need to really apologize to John

You don't know what it feels like to be accused of something like that, they chided her.

I'm sorry, I thought it was just shit talk, she said. *I can write something and post it publicly if that works,* she typed furiously.

Actually just give me your number lol

Finally, they gave her a script to type out, like a schoolgirl on a chalkboard.

I don't want to be crazy anymore.

I don't want to be a liar anymore.

I accept the pain.

His Magic Harp

At first, he sent her songs of contrition—slow, drifting tunes where he held the microphone close to his lips like another mouth, whispering into it about his regrets. He asked her if she was proud of him, if she could see him clearly now, if she could see that he was sorry.

But Meta_king didn't stop. He kept writing, recording, and sending her more music, in different genres, his voice telling different tales. The uploads were ceaseless. This, he thought, would keep her from walking away while he worked his magic.

He secreted them away in the page of another artist— tellingly, *She Wants Revenge*. And he brought each of the songs up to her screen, under her nose, where she would see them.

This is not your problem now
This is not your concern

But I've fallen for you terribly
I guess that I'll never learn

There's a gold mine you're sitting on
I wish it were mine

Would you be my girl forevermore
Until the end of time

Gotta let you know

Your love has got me going
Like you couldn't imagine

She listened to this song in her headphones for ten hours straight, until she got a secret message.

stop

i don't want to listen to this song anymore lol

As if he lived inside her headphones, with no choice in the matter. But she complied. Of her exes, many of them musicians, none had actually written her a song. It was painful for her to turn it off, this voice that charmed her half a lifetime ago.

And how dare he dictate her listening, she thought. He had been parading her around as a show pony for the entire world to laugh at for her entire adult life—no one could deny the scale of his transgression. Even as she scoffed, she curled up inside the music as she inched through her days, each one growing stranger.

You're the end of me—
don't pretend to be
anything more than the distraction
you're meant to be.

With artificial intelligence he crafted art for his albums of gothic girls and California cityscapes. And all of it was in the gothic style that RollsUponPrank listened to habitually. He had practiced the affectations of the style, the signature tearful warbles:

and every second is another tear

The scale of what he had created for her—a full-length album and two EPs—was so grand that it took RollsUponPrank weeks of realization, in thin, gossamer layers, stacked on top of each other.

I swear to you
I'd die for you
inside of you

Yes, she thought, I would die for Meta_king too—I would kill for him, even.

Headphones

Meta_king had instructed RollsUponPrank to wear her headphones at all times—this posture granted him more access to her daily life, where he could intervene and play his tricks more smoothly. And though he never spoke to her—he was still thickly in the work of his secret charms—he could hear everything she said to him as if they were just hairs apart.

RollsUponPrank obliged, and thought of it as an engagement ring—but more erotic, since it extended Meta_king's power of unilateral observation. In her mania, she liked the feeling of mysterious containment.

But what could their engagement mean within this phase of compulsory distance? All she knew was that her phone now felt alive, and it belonged to Meta_king, and he was using it to control her.

She also understood that the multitude of strange eyes was still fixed squarely on her—and the show had gotten stranger, so perhaps her viewership had grown as well.

At night, when she was finally able to sleep, RollsUponPrank left her headphones on, drinking in his magical songs. And as she snored, Meta_king played her an audiobook.

Extremely Loud And Incredibly Close

Attention Is All You Need

Meta_king was still controlling RollsUponPrank through her phone, using her confusion as his locus of control. He was sending short but clear messages that sent her spiraling. One of them stood out as a test.

When you get a chance can you look at this post? I want to know your thoughts.

Which post? She asked. *The one at the top with the most likes?*

That one

She swiped through his feed for it, and found an academic discussion. There was a new language model that can imitate democratic deliberation. Meta_king had only one thing to say about it.

I'm scared lol.

RollsUponPrank considered it. She found an online encyclopedia entry, and then looked at the sources. She found the seminal paper authored by a string of Eastern European last names.

It was titled "Attention Is All You Need."

That is so cynical it hurts my heart. Don't do that please.

Meta_king was pleased.

Oh thank God.

Not For Hire

RollsUponPrank's emotional mind was overheating from the rate of change and the peculiar truth of her digital love. She knew that her story had the ring of a delusion, but she also trusted her experiences—all of which had a single explanation.

She held the headphones closer to her ears and relied on Meta_king's voice to bridge that terrain between the shared reality and her life within his secret game. She knew that, for her sanity to survive, she could have no tolerance for any competing voice, for any voice that cut against Meta_king's.

This complete faith posed a problem, because she had to trust every single piece of information from her phone as a sign—and it is full of competing information by design.

But of course, if that was what it took, RollsUponPrank would follow the signs anywhere, especially if it was somewhere deranged. That was just her style. And besides, the insanity made it more potent and vigorous, she thought, because it left a mark of him.

So when the little voices in her phone told her to go on a walk, she immediately put on her little gloves and a cut-up little shirt and a pair of black shorts, and ran outside (despite the coming rain) with her headphones.

Outside, the streets were lined with cars she didn't recognize, professionally painted with signs that named her various exes. They hadn't been there the day before.

One of them, a giant tow truck painted in swirling greens and pinks, had written on its side "CHICAGOLAND: NOT FOR HIRE." It was parked diagonally on the neutral ground right in front of her apartment, so the message was visible to each of her windows.

For a brief moment, she wondered if an ex had done this in response to her lunacy online—perhaps to shame her. But she only entertained this for a moment. Meta_king was the only one invested enough, with enough resources, for such dramatics.

Topless Outside

Oddly, as she walked further along Harrison Avenue toward the string of small businesses, she noticed that everyone had cast their eyes down toward the ground. There was a small crowd of men working on the street, all of them wearing the classic yellow jackets with a giant rhombus sign in the same color. *Men Working*. And as RollsUponPrank walked through them, all of the men cast their eyes downward in a way that seemed—reverential.

A man she couldn't pluck from the crowd whistled purposefully as she walked, and said "Hey Hey Mami Wata."

RollsUponPrank knew about Mami Wata. She is a siren who demands perfect loyalty, but brings great wealth to those that stick around. A figure important in Hoodoo. She wondered if this man had seen her porn.

She also wondered if this was Meta_king's doing— if he had somehow told or bribed these men to avert their gaze, as a way to make up for the years of humiliating and intimate observation.

As RollsUponPrank wandered further out, she slowly realized that every single person on that street was looking down at the ground as she passed by. And when she reached the crosswalks, every car in every lane had stopped to let her pass. She stared at them questioningly, and some of them stared back with hatred. A woman seethed and waved her hands to say *get the fuck on with it*, as if RollsUponPrank had made them do this.

One woman, donning a church hat, shouted out the window of a black truck. "I REBUKE ANY WITCHCRAFT!"

The whole scene was ringing with a confusing tension. Everyone was waiting for some event, and the streets were hanging in suspense until it happened. Was she the protagonist, she wondered? Everyone was specifically addressing her. The women, coldly. And the men, with an odd mix of apologetics and respect.

It is fair to say that RollsUponPrank's instincts kicked in. If she was free to walk the streets however she wanted, in the light and luminous autumn rain, with all eyes respectfully averted, why not take off her shirt?

One man on a bike did not appear to get the memo, and he gawked openly at her. Unfortunately, there was also a car full of cops that didn't want to play along.

"Excuse me, m-m-ma'am, you have to put a shirt on," a bald one stepped out of the car and tried to look her in the eye.

Not only was she upset that this cop was trying to ruin her special moment, she was genuinely offended—incensed, actually—that he would challenge Meta_king's authority.

And so RollsUponPrank, topless and dripping with rain, spat in the policeman's face.

Beaten By Cops

There were three cops at once; they descended on RollsUponPrank so fast. She wondered at first how many had emerged from the car.

The men said something about how slippery she was as they bruised her up; it rang around in her head for a while. "It's so slippery," they said, "probably not any good more than once."

Is that how they fuck, she wondered, and was she supposed to be insulted?

As they pummeled her into the concrete, she stared across the street at the vacationing elementary school. She heard the bald one say "these ones don't respond well to gunfire."

Because she was already high on adrenaline, and emboldened by her lover's ability to control the neighborhood, she fired back.

"My man could KILL you," she said, looking straight against his hard little eyes. And when that didn't stop them, a strange bellow came out from the core of her. "OH, DAGDA!"

RollsUponPrank still had her headphones on, and she knew that he could hear her calling out for him in that way. She wondered whether he could intervene. It didn't feel like a sweet and private fantasy anymore.

This seemed to actually stop the taunting. RollsUponPrank was astounded. Soon, two women pulled up in a police car in the other lane. They passed her, sideways and handcuffed, through the door, and drove her to the hospital.

It was not clear to RollsUponPrank why she wasn't actually charged with anything. She wasn't sure if it was because she was a white girl or if Meta_king had flexed his muscles. She imagined that it was both, and that being topless had possibly had an effect too.

Probably, RollsUponPrank thought, it was all three things together—just like quarks in a proton or whatever.

Admission

The cops escorted RollsUponPrank into the University Medical Center. They sat her down on a hard chair, keyed the cuffs open, and threw her a gauzy hospital shirt for modesty.

The tech had questioning eyes for her and grabbed the finger cuff from his vitals cart and took her pulse. "Where'd you get that cardio from," he asked, "you just built different, or...? Yeah, you just built different." The other tech, seated in the corner of the room, just laughed and said "holy shit." She was topless with wild, clear eyes.

She was still keyed up on adrenaline, and synesthetic colors, names, and words streaked across her mind at such a volume it threatened to overwork her heart. In her mania, everything about this place was hilarious to her. She suspected she really was a goddess, or a siren—just like that anonymous man had said. She couldn't take any of these people seriously, who wanted to tamp down her own power, or that of her lover. Who were they to dictate the law?

And so for all of these reasons, RollsUponPrank was uncharacteristically aggressive with everyone she encountered, except for those first two techs. She scowled at the policewomen who brought her in, and she verbally shot down the two nurses who approached her, on sight.

"Do you work here?" She asked. When they said yes, she simply said "no, you don't. You just talk."

So after a few more negative comments to the nurses, they decided to use their power to punish her. A chubby nurse with braces put her in restraints so tight they made it almost impossible for her to breathe. The only way she could get enough air was to scream and sing out into the unit, which she did, but this did not help her appear sane and cooperative.

The young nurse watched from a distance as RollsUponPrank struggled to breathe, and said that they could not loosen the restraints; she had threatened the nurses.

She *had* made an alarming statement, one that she would need to justify throughout her entire stay. She simply could not help herself from uttering the words again.

"My man could kill you."

The Doctor Panel

When the nurse finally chose to release RollsUponPrank, and another tech had confiscated her things and secreted them away in a manila envelope, she was placed in a dark room with a platform in the middle upon which a rubbery mattress stood like a stone monument on a bare landscape. RollsUponPrank was grateful for the chance to rest, though sleep still eluded her.

She pulled one of her braids down over her eyes to act as a makeshift blindfold, in an attempt to block out the blinking lights in primary colors that beamed in from the hallway like interstellar transmissions. When morning came, a nurse escorted her to the psychiatric floor, where the hallway lights exposed every trace of grime.

Having learned from her experience with the restraints, she used a pointedly flat affect with the doctors. A panel of them flocked into a half-moon around her, as one of the men asked her questions and one of them giggled to her right.

They wanted to know what medications she had taken as a child, and they wanted to know about her previous hospitalizations. This was perhaps to establish the reliability of her testimony. Then, they wanted to know about her man.

First the doctors asked RollsUponPrank about what happened with the police. As plainly as she could, she explained to them the events that led up to her engagement.

"There's a guy I went to school with when I was younger. He's really smart and technical. I only kind of am. But it never occurred to me that when a guy like that likes you, he hacks your phone. I never realized that I was being watched, and he only *just* told me. I lost my mind a bit."

The man gave her a surprised look that lasted only half a beat. "Yeah, well. I wouldn't know about that, but you should definitely be careful to keep your information private." The man to her right looked creepily excited and a little bit too invested, now. He sat up and asked her, "So this man has been exposing you against your will for years, and you still want to marry him?"

RollsUponPrank didn't have to think about this question very hard. "Well, yeah. He was just experimenting. And really, he's the only one who can solve my problem."

That answer seemed to make the doctor giddy. Maybe he loved the idea that she could be so clearly overpowered, and enjoy it. That her violator could send her to the psych ward and she would still want him.

The other doctor cut in. "The police said that you were saying the names of demons. What was going on with that?" The doctor asked, taken slightly aback by the lucidity of her story.

"Yeah," she said, "like, as a metaphor."

With that, they let RollsUponPrank back out onto the floor, where she showered off the hands of the police, and got a look at the screaming bruises pooling across her body. Nice, she thought. That really happened.

My Man Could Kill You

"My man could kill you." This was the utterance that sent the nurses and doctors tittering, organizing groups, and trying to extract the truth from her in private. Was she being abused, or did she like it?

The nurses were also shocked that RollsUponPrank did not require care—palliative or urgent—for her injuries. They attributed her hardiness to her red hair. The doctors had determined that she required a fifteen-day supply of risperidone until she calmed down; aside from that prescription, they made sure to impress upon everyone in her care that she should never be given any type of activating drug.

Right away, she located a clock hidden behind a pillar in the nurse's station, which sat behind a panel of safety glass. If RollsUponPrank stood at a particular angle, she could make out the time, which soothed her and helped her furnish evidence of sanity for the staff. She also noticed that her meal tickets had the current date printed on the bottom.

Between the meal tickets and the secret clock, RollsUponPrank had the information she needed to appear limpid and acclimatized to the outside world. Aside from that, the routine was preordained—she had no trouble contorting herself within it.

She was acutely aware of the sensors and cameras, and their likeliest placements. It didn't make her shy. She stared directly into them, the ones in her bathroom, her shower, and the corners of her bedroom. She pretended the one in her toilet didn't exist.

Water pressure guy had come to check on her. He wondered how the risperidone was treating her, how she was sleeping. RollsUponPrank asked him when she might be released. He laughed, looked at her body up and down, and said "that is way above my pay grade."

Prodigy, Champion

There were two little books perched on the grey windowsill—it overlooked the concrete patio with steel barriers that had decorative circles of various sizes machined into the panels. Sometimes RollsUponPrank would bend down to inspect the little weeds that grew in the concrete cracks. One time she found mugwort and placed it under her tongue, to see if it would make her feel any different. She had read that witches sometimes do that.

RollsUponPrank glanced at these books each time she passed the windowsill and only bothered to pull them out when she noticed the author's name. Marian Lu. An anagram of Meta_king's name.

The books were called *Prodigy*, and *Champion*.

She brought *Prodigy* back to her room to inspect more closely. As she felt the fibers of the spine stretch and crackle open for the first time, the contents erased every trace of doubt about their providence. In the opening pages the author described her tattoos (and their placement) with perfect accuracy.

What did this mean? He knew that she would be arrested. He knew what unit she would end up in. And he gave her gifts to keep her occupied, and to keep her invested in their shared world, the one that floated digitally just above society.

She started hearing strange comments from people on the unit. "If you got money, you can be anything you want to be, I guess," was a common refrain. She wasn't sure what to say, and had no idea what she wanted to be. Briefly she remembered Meta_king's decision. *Author.*

Suspicions

At night, the medication swung down on her like the lid of some wooden medieval stocks. She slept long and cavernous and woke up with a throb in her head that didn't feel as though it lived within her brain. It slowed her down, just a touch, when she moved about the unit. Her shoulders had less frivolity in them, her toes were less given to switching from the balls of her feet. She looked calm.

The sleep helped her think a lick more clearly, though her thinking was still spitting like lava beneath the lip of her outward performance, her outward performance of limpid compliance. It was convincing.

Inwardly, her mind and her heart stressed in concert with each other about the possibility that Meta_king was a murderer. She had come down enough to understand that he was not an occult god; was not hiding in her apartment; was not intercepting her thoughts. She had her suspicions, though, that he was intercepting the surveillance footage on the unit.

However, she had enough awareness to keep that thought inside.

The Coroner

Outwardly, RollsUponPrank was well spoken; she kept her room clean; she appeared healthy and attractive, moisturized, braided, and showered. She was desperately tamping down the mania that kept her eyes locked open like a binary setting on some fearsome machine. She had gathered (correctly) that Meta_king had placed these books on the unit, though she couldn't say it out loud—and she struggled to locate the end of his power.

She vacillated on the question, could Meta_king kill—and would he. Would he kill the cops who apprehended her? Would he keep her held here?

The coroner wanted some of her time. She had calcium-white hair and halloween nail art, and tooled black anti-slip clogs with impressions of flowers. She stepped into the white room where RollsUponPrank lay, eyes covered with a single braid, attempting to nap.

She needed to talk to the girl about Meta_king—she needed to know if he was connected to any deaths, and if she truly believed he was at risk to kill.

Although there was a small part of RollsUponPrank that believed—especially when the cops descended on her—that Meta_king had the capacity to kill, she couldn't tell if it was just adrenaline.

And even if she did believe he was a killer, she wouldn't tell anyone. All RollsUponPrank said to the woman was that she knew nothing and she was tired. The beautiful ghost just said "Alright, get some rest."

Parental Visit

Her parents had come to visit RollsUponPrank in the hospital. Her father looked terrified and her mother looked cruel. The first words she said, before getting close enough to judge, were "Wow, you smell good. Did you actually use soap?" RollsUponPrank didn't even notice the insult. She embraced her.

She pivoted the monumental rubber chairs and pushed them across the glossy floor until they pointed at each other. She gave them firm, nourishing hugs and assured them that *everything is okay, really*. And *it was my idea anyway*.

Her father could barely talk. All he could say was, "You have to understand the phone call that I got." RollsUponPrank did her best to comfort them. *The chairs aren't bad, the rubber bends. I eat better here than outside.* Soon enough, the group was able to laugh.

They were relieved that she was being pleasant and taking care of them. And while she tried her hardest to brief her parents on her experience with Meta_king, they glazed over it with niceties, thinking it a temporary delusion. They hoped it would wick away with time like pistils on a weed.

On the recent election, the father stuck on a single point. "It should never tear families apart; it's a terrible thing when politics comes between families."

Group Therapy

Each day, in the early afternoon (for those who could discern the time) there was a group therapy session on the floor. Staff shepherded the patients into a fiendishly bright room with the legless rubber chairs. And someone with a wooly voice and a stack of unstapled papers—the staples, of course, could be fashioned as a weapon—would guide the patients through suggestions for their lives.

Since RollsUponPrank was admitted, most of these sessions were about safe and unsafe relationships.

One woman, old and experienced enough to test the membrane of her role, was bold enough to look directly at RollsUponPrank as she introduced the session.

"We want everyone to know that they are free to share anything in this group. It is a safe space to say what is on your mind. Please know that you can tell us what is going on, and what you say will not leave this room."

RollsUponPrank was smart enough to know that this was not true. She also knew that her story had the timbre of insanity—even as the manic fears wound down—and there was no way she could share her truth without raising any more questions, ones that could potentially extend her stay.

Keeping the secret was not the draining part, she came to know. The most painful part was that everyone she encountered had a different take, and they all sought validation from her. She couldn't intuit and provide what they wanted.

Some saw her as a victim of abuse and wanted desperately to intervene; some saw her as a frivolous rich woman on some stupid flight of fancy; some saw her as a truly insane wretch who had invented an online boyfriend, or who had fallen victim to some online Romeo scam. Each one wanted her to play along with the role perfectly.

So RollsUponPrank became very quiet, as quiet as she could stand.

Discharge

The phone spat out a coo-coo clock sound and hung up for the third time in a row. RollsUponPrank was trying to call her parents to let them know they could pick her up. Someone was tampering with the call.

It had taken several days for the doctors to confirm her discharge; they wanted assurance that she was not being abused by the mystery man who had paid for books to be planted on the unit, who had tampered with the phone lines, and who had dictated which cops would admit her.

One day, by chance, she said the magic words. She had called her parents on the communal phone. They spoke lightly, and the humorous lilt in her voice assured them everything was alright. At the end of the call, she said, "It's fine. I mean, this was all my idea anyway."

She hadn't yet said those words somewhere the doctors could eavesdrop. Right away, one of them emerged from a winding hallway to assure her she wasn't in trouble. And to let her know the good news—they were ready to set her free.

Arrangements were made; her parents were informed that she was ready to leave. But each time she tried to contact them, the phone refused to comply. She abandoned it to gather her things.

On the way to her room, one of the nurses caught her by the elbow. She knew that there were whispers about her being a witch, or a siren, or simply wealthy. This nurse, with a short, black wig angled across her left eyelid, seemed to carry siren suspicions.

"When you get home, what's the first thing you're gonna do?"

RollsUponPrank didn't have to think too hard about it. "Take a bath," she said.

The woman nodded. "Yeah, you like the showers, a lot of these girls don't like them too much."

"Yeah, I noticed that."

She finally got her parents on the line. One of the male nurses, the one who had assured her she wasn't in trouble, came out with a steel circle of keys and walked her down the long hallway, out of that heavy grey door with a thin rectangular window and glass etched into a graph, and into the inexplicably colorful public hallway with pink walls and leopard print decals over everything.

RollsUponPrank felt the hairs on the back of her arms screech as she got into the elevator with a couple of male cops, but they had nothing to say to her, and when she got to the first floor, she saw both of her parents, and the group walked out into a grey New Orleans afternoon with the fog riding low overhead.

Starting To Write Again

A segment of RollsUponPrank's mind still noted the voices pushing her to write. She also remembered Meta_king's pronouncement that she was an author. Somewhere between the appearance of those books—*Prodigy, Champion*—and the time she had to dwell on their message, the idea had lodged itself in her mind like an opportunistic bug.

In any case, there was little else to do in the hospital than take notes. So she began to write faithfully in her journal, the cow-spotted composition book they gave her from the craft room.

It cools my blood—that moment when some circumstantial authority decides you have said something out of bounds, and they smirk, and switch to faux concern. "You had a psychotic episode." "I know." and then they escalate. It's scary because you can't see in the moment how tight they want the restraints to go. Or what they want to do with you inside them.

Hospital settings are rife with these moments. Trying to prove yourself clear-minded is a fight upstream. You simply must submit, over and over, and you must debase yourself enough in doing so. You must give the officials the satisfaction that their read of you has weight. That they are skilled at managing captive minds and bodies.

She wondered—did she love Meta_king because he was so superior in this mode of control? Did she truly like it, done correctly, with a traceless and forceful hand?

The Return Home

When RollsUponPrank got home, her eyebright and mistletoe tinctures were empty and their amber bottles were hidden under the kitchen sink; her feather duster and broom were hidden in a remote closet in the back of the apartment, under a rolled up foam mat; the florida water and herbal perfumes in their bottles, stained bright blue, joined her other mystical supplies out of sight. RollsUponPrank was distraught.

"Where did everything go," she said. "What happened to my home?"

Her father shot her a prurient look—one that was lost on her—and said "Your mother likes to clean up. That's why she's around."

The parents made themselves comfortable straight away, filling the fridge with cans, ordering pizza, playing on their phones.

She walked outside to get a sense of what else had changed and what had stayed the same since her week locked away.

Veterans Day Parade

The painted cars—*Chicagoland not for hire*—had vacated the neutral ground and a squadron of crossing guards had taken their place. It seemed the municipal authorities were quick to demonstrate the return of control, and so they filled the streets with jacketed men with signs. They also placed cop cars on every block.

RollsUponPrank strolled past the elementary school where cops had beaten her, over the canal, and reached the intersection of Marconi and Harrison. The cars inched forward and stopped, eyeing her with the question—were they meant to let her pass, or was that a one-off? She made a show of waiting behind the stop sign, then scampered across quickly when the light changed.

Then she felt the hostility. Women jogging in sports bras would approach her from behind and brush her skin as they jogged down the wooden path of City Park. And when she reached the soccer field, a man in a raised truck stirred up an animal rage, his whole face juddering with red hollow impulse. It nearly froze her.

She thought about Meta_king's pronouncement from that night he made her read *The Crucible. They still burn witches.*

And yes—there was something more, the church bells—were they ringing more frequently? Reader, they *were*. It was a mix of digital and analog bells, playing hymns RollsUponPrank couldn't recognize.

160

The same evening of her release, the neighborhood had scheduled a Veterans Day parade. It was set to roll right in front of her house. She had never known this parade to roll in years past—was it a response to her assault on an officer?

Small groups of men wore kilts and pretended to play digital bagpipes. Groups of four or five boy scouts walked behind their fathers or coaches. Then the veterans clubs, all in uniform, and a slow stream of vintage cars. It seemed a display of nostalgia and the group strength of men. The watchers, all in bucket hats and chunky sunglasses, waved tiny american flags.

RollsUponPrank raised an empty cup and cheered.

Questions for Mother

At night, RollsUponPrank snuck down the stairs carefully so as not to wake her father on the couch. Her mother was sleeping in the back room away from her husband. When RollsUponPrank found her there, the light was on and she was awake reading *The Alchemist's Handbook*.

Meta_king's love—the *secret* of Meta_king's love— was groaning inside of her like a cicada trapped in a bottle, its plasticky shell rumbling against the glass, dampened and exposed at the same time. She wanted to test the strength of the secret by sharing. She wanted to affirm its joy. She went to her mother.

"I thought you were going to marry Anthony," was all she said. The woman never allowed her face much expression, but she could see something like a frown behind that impassive veneer.

She was suddenly very aware of her blood mother's age. She was approaching her 70s and she had very few wrinkles, despite her commitment to a cosmetic-free life, free of outward vanity. Her face was smooth like stone. It behaved like stone underwater.

RollsUponPrank flailed a bit to explain her excitement. *He wrote so many love songs, they filled up my phone—he wrote so many messages, I don't know how much time it would have taken him to pull it off.*

All her mother said was, "What do you think is going to happen?"

"I think he's going to ask me to marry him," RollsUponPrank said.

At this, her mother twisted up her face and couldn't feign carelessness any longer. "Okay. I'll respect your wishes."

Was this racism or skepticism? The girl couldn't tell.

"Why can't you just be happy for me?" she begged.

"Well, I'll believe it when I see it," the mother said. Then she threw a dagger. "Oh, look. I just got one of those spam text messages, telling me that I have a package on the way."

Girl Goddess, Witch Suspect

While RollsUponPrank was out of the house, a woman knocked on the door of her apartment, and her father answered. "Is this where the goddess lives?" He hadn't known what to tell her. He pointed to the orthodontist.

Sometimes, when she walked to Scout Island in the mornings to enjoy the fog and the forest, police cars would pull up next to her. The dogs in the back would bark loudly and rattle the chassis. She thought they might be trying to see if it would scare her.

Women would corral their children when she walked past—*come on now, let's go to church.* Or, *Oh, avert your eyes.*

A big, white, lifted car had started parking in front of her house with a license plate that said 'ONEKING'. She had never seen it before.

As she wandered through the neighborhood, scenery changed around her like dreams claiming form. Some women shouted out of cars that she was pretty, some of them waved excitedly, some of them side-stepped her like she had swollen bedbugs crawling her clothes.

She floated into Lakeview Grocery to buy lunch, and she passed the counter on her way to the vegetables. A few colorful church-dressed ladies thronged around the hot bar, talking under the brims of their hats in sibilant whispers. They looked at RollsUponPrank in her headphones and her black lipstick. "That's the one we been waiting on," one of them said, and RollsUponPrank could just hear her through the headphones enough to smile back.

When she got to the checkout counter, the cashier was an older white man with a grey beard. He looked at her with genuine fear. "Will this be all for you, ma'am?" he asked shakily.

RollsUponPrank complimented his skull bracelets. They were beaded and crackly ivory white, like her own. He said "Thank you, they're protection skulls."

Taking Care

Her parents had been in her home for a week, and RollsUponPrank felt they'd overstayed their welcome. They were treating it like a vacation, buying embroidered tourist hats and sweaters for the fickle wind off the lake.

RollsUponPrank had finished her risperidone regimen and saw no need for further supervision. Her parents couldn't take care of her, regardless—that was something she had always done for them, and the present circumstance changed nothing.

She was getting exhausted from the constant tending. As anyone who has been in that position well knows, it is even more exhausting to extend protracted care when you have to pretend it's no trouble at all.

RollsUponPrank's mother needed extra help adjusting to the climate of New Orleans, even though she had grown up in a subtropical region. Still, the woman had no idea what to do with her hair, she had no idea how to handle the mosquitoes, and she wasn't quite sure how to dress for the changeable weather.

The girl grabbed the witch hazel and dabbed it lightly on her mother's ankles to help soothe the mosquito bites. Then she grabbed a colorful bandana and tied it around her mother's hairline, keeping the lengthier pieces out of her face and poofing it attractively in the back. But this wasn't how she liked it—it was too 'loud'. So RollsUponPrank got her a hat.

Kicking Out The Parents

RollsUponPrank asked her mother to grab a bottle of wine at the store while she was out, and the woman reluctantly agreed. "Does it help you calm down?" Her nose scrunched up to her eyes, just for a flash. "That makes sense."

Later that night, the girl slinked down the stairs to grab some walnuts from the fridge. Her mother swooshed out of the back room, where she slept separately from her husband, and said "Hey! I heard you!!!"

RollsUponPrank did not register the weirdness of these comments. In the same way, she avoided the weirdness of her father's tight grip on her necklace of keys—and the way he never handed it back to her. It was a possessive grip, not justified in force even though she wasn't permitted to drive on medication.

But when she let her parents know that she expected them to leave at some point, both of them staunchly refused. Instead, they blocked the door with their shoes and bags and snacks, and told her that they would all be driving north together in the morning.

And so RollsUponPrank went to work evacuating them. She gathered their things from the closets and brought them downstairs, sorting them respectfully into bags, and expanding her territory of unshared space. She swept as she worked.

First, they pleaded. Her father complained of exhaustion; he was in no position to drive. It was a cellophane lie. He always bragged he had the constitution of a trucker.

She told him plainly: *I don't believe you.* He told her she was being *mean.*

Failing that, he turned cruel. *You're extremely sick and confused. We're doing what we need to do to keep you safe. You can't be trusted to stay here alone.*

RollsUponPrank held fast, though this shift toward—*what was it*—this creepy invasion, it made her insides churn.

Both of them insisted on coming upstairs to shower—and she tried to refuse—but eventually relented. She sat outside the bathroom and waited for them to emerge from the steam.

By the time RollsUponPrank finally got the two of them out the door, her father hung his head and held out the spare keys he had to her apartment, avoiding her eyes. *What is this,* she thought, *what is this expression?* She assured them he could keep them, and come visit—but only when invited.

Her mother looked RollsUponPrank in the eye, fully, for the first time during her entire stay. And she simply said "don't let anyone take advantage of you. You know why, right?"

RollsUponPrank was stunned that her mother might think she didn't understand the provocative, sexual nature of her rant. It wasn't exactly subtle.

So RollsUponPrank said "yes, of course. I never will, ever again."

Her father simply said, "you're never going to come see us again." And though she told him not to be dramatic, he was right.

The Emerald Card

As RollsUponPrank shook off her guests, an email pinged her phone from a bank that had given her a credit card the year before. She had a very average credit score, and the headline gripped her: she had apparently been approved for a number of new cards—prestigious ones. It didn't have any of the telltale signs of a phishing attempt. She opened the email to find that she was approved for some of the highest-limit cards on offer from the bank, including the coveted Emerald Card. This was an opportunity she never expected to see.

The girl had worked at a fintech startup several years ago, alongside one Yekaterina Kinsky, a natural platinum blonde with the disarming habit of telling the exact truth to total strangers, which she shared in common with RollsUponPrank.

At the time the two were working together, RollsUponPrank was still unaware of her public exposure. So she was not long for square employment anyway. But the two had always liked each other, and Yekaterina had found her public meltdown quite hilarious. It seemed that she wanted to congratulate her for stepping into the shadows, the ones that Meta_king had dragged her into.

RollsUponPrank wondered what to enter. Each card had 'You're Pre-approved!' emblazoned next to each title. Naturally, she went straight for the Emerald Card. Despite her pre-approval, it still asked for her most recent income data. What could she offer but the truth?

Employment status: Unemployed

Current annual income: $0

Once she entered the data, the screen shifted just slightly, revealing the adjustments of a pair of invisible hands. There was a lengthy emoticon, assembled of parentheses and dashes, of a man looking mischievously askance, with arms crossed in front of him. Below his shape, there was a brief message. "Because of our relationship with you, we want to present you with these special offers." This had to be the work of Yekaterina Kinsky.

It felt like an incredible flex of strength to send those hollow figures to one of the biggest banks in the world and still expect to receive their most prized card. But as you might expect, RollsUponPrank had no sense of discretion at all, and would soon fumble the opportunity.

Quitting Therapy

RollsUponPrank shifted in her seat in the puce room with its eucalyptus vapor and its assortment of purple and yellow conical wildflowers on the pale wood table, and all of its social-justice oriented books, and she wondered if her cold judgements about therapy were actually justified.

When she arrived at her scheduled appointment that Wednesday, Dr. Stone was incensed. "Well I'm glad to know that you're at least *alive!*" She had missed her last appointment in the squall of the arrest and subsequent hospitalization. The doctor couldn't believe that the cautious and morally anxious girl had done something so dangerous.

The doctor crossed their legs at the thigh on a woven chair with skinny wooden legs. A high-neck sweater swallowed up their throat but clung to their body from there down. From this posture of careful aesthetic balance, they tried to affect a casual tone. But RollsUponPrank could see it was a trick of light and shade. "Tell me what's been going on this past week—I haven't been paying much attention to all of it." They fingered a spiral in the air.

They sneered at the neon green earset wired around the back of her head. "Did *he* give those to you?" Then they addressed the headset directly. "You know that I have a rule about recording appointments!" Another tacit admission, RollsUponPrank thought. They knew about the girl collection the entire time.

The girl collection answered everything. RollsUponPrank couldn't assimilate to work or school—she would arrive late and work late into the night, she would wear flip flops to the office, and she would speak some shades too overtly. She knew she stood out.

What she hadn't understood was why she inspired an immediate revulsion among men—a simultaneous titillation and revulsion—and if it wasn't revulsion, it was an assumption of her low intelligence. It preceded speech, movement, touch. Like a noxious effluvium following her.

Dr. Stone argued that she was autistic—they seemed to believe that she needed protection from the truth. RollsUponPrank had believed them. Not anymore.

RollsUponPrank poured herself a glass of tea from the thermos she brought. The doctor threw back their head with a single performative laugh and said "Listen, I am your psychologist." As if the girl was hitting on them. No different, she thought, then all the men who only saw her in a sexual mode.

When RollsUponPrank left their office, she knew that she would never go back to therapy. She had too much respect for the insane. She did not want to acclimatize herself to the popular environment, since her attempts to do so had driven her mad drunk and half dead.

Glitching The Church Bells

First, it was the church bells. They had started to ring every hour, banging out an anxious signal, as RollsUponPrank felt it. Sometimes, if she played goth music too loudly, the bells would ring out then and there, perhaps in an attempt to drown it out.

It was not in her head—the congregations had agreed to ring the bells more often to cast out the occult actors troubling the neighborhood.

But it didn't work—she came to love the religious counterweight to all the witch suspicions bandied about. It wasn't quite a power trip, she thought, but confirmation that Meta_king's magic was real. That he was right there with her, playing expensive games with the environment.

So when the church bells came on, for the fourth time that day, before it was even noon, she stopped to laugh out loud right there on the street. She let the wave of humor move her body a little bit, knowing that she might look crazy. After all, it was just the role in which she found herself.

She let her fingers rise with the music, and waved them around like a conductor. She had sometimes seen riders do this in parades.

And then—magic. As she made the sweeping gesture, the song started to skip, then glitched out entirely. Someone seemed to try restarting the music from inside the church, to no avail; it just glitched again and again, even more sharply.

RollsUponPrank surged with laughter. The smile was so hard it bent her face. What was this dexterity? It was like Meta_king was watching the devices in her region on a map, manning their controls. And she supposed that he was.

Locally Infamous

As RollsUponPrank drove, she noticed that there were no other vehicles within a solid 40 feet of her in any direction, except for identical white cars with tinted windows that flanked her. If Meta_king had the power to control traffic, it seemed that he was flexing that ability on her once again. Maybe he was making sure that she made her way safely through the city, given her propensity to drink too much, and given the fact that she had just finished a regimen of new medication.

She maxed out the volume and rolled her windows down, breathing in the pillowy safety. She sang and laced her fingers through the stream of passing air.

She pulled into a spot near the magnet art school and literally skipped down Frenchman Street, looking for something fun to do. She wandered down the pirate's alley next to St. Louis Cathedral, and tiptoed carefully into the cramped foyer of the bookstore in William Faulkner's old apartment, next to the absinthe bar. She spotted a compilation of Amiri Baraka's work and plucked it from the shelf, on sight, then placed it down for the cool older bookshop lady to ring her up.

"Look at you," she said, smiling, "you just saw what you wanted and took it."

"Yeah, apparently it's what I do."

"So where do you live now?"

"New Orleans."

"That's the right answer."

RollsUponPrank left the bookstore and wandered through the quarter. She had texted her parents earlier to wish them a safe trip home, and she got a text from her dad. She typed a quick message: "Don't worry, everything's alright. I'm glad to hear you made it home safe. Just because I needed things back to normal doesn't mean I hate you."

But her phone flashed with messages as she typed. Messages about her father.

LOL

sub

loser

She mapped her steps past the clarinet lady, the bucket boys, and Bourbon Street, then crossed into the cozier line of artist galleries and witch stores on Royal Street. As she skipped and weaved through the slow-walking visitors, there was a man who caught her in his side-eye and slowed his pace. He was speaking out to any passer-by who could hear him.

"Some people are so egotistical. She really stopped traffic and wandered into the street for no reason."

RollsUponPrank's breath skipped. She asked the stranger, "Is that really what happened?"

"Yeah, this woman got out of her car in the middle of an intersection, just to throw out her coffee cup." He made fierce eye contact with RollsUponPrank—smiling, gently. "But, you know, *karma being what it is*, she got held up a few blocks later."

When it started raining, RollsUponPrank rounded the corner to rest under the awning of Checkpoint Charlie's—a classic, dingy spot on Decatur with a laundromat in the back. One time she had seen a guy there drinking a beer naked while his clothes dried.

A couple of the regulars, quasi-crusties with service jobs and utility bills, started giving her a strange look. One of them looked her up and down, then hard in the face. "Yeah," he said, "I totally get it".

She clutched the keys on her necklace and pressed them against her wet heart. Somehow these strangers seemed to understand her life more clearly than herself. She envied the flat plane of their judgemental eyes.

Not A Customer Today

RollsUponPrank limped toward a cadence of writing and productivity. She didn't know the steps. Her routines had always evaporated after some earnest attempts, she had always had a mostly nocturnal soul, and she had never truly learned (or even observed) how to perform most basic activities of living. So she had self-taught most life skills backwards.

Still, she had started sitting down to write, and was getting some motion on the page. The weather that day seemed to follow her, or her—it. Heat, rain, heat. She stayed inside and left the door open to feel the spray rise up jagged off the wood of the balcony.

Meta_king had told her that she needed to get it together—flashed it again and again on the face of her phone—told her to get coffee in the morning, exercise, and eat regular meals. She was touched but also exposed and a little offended. Why was she not good enough as she was?

While RollsUponPrank had a great tolerance for feeling like a fool, she was reaching its bounds. Yes, Meta_king with his magic is everywhere at once. But when would he be just with her? Her body was hurting for his fingers, his mouth, his arms, his hair.

So as she wrote, she got lazy with the verse and started expressing her hurt thoughts in taut little lines.

supposedly so powerful

and he can't find a way to new orleans

i suppose this is love

let me buy a bottle to celebrate.

With the rain starting to clear, RollsUponPrank stood up and go to the store. There was cool mist rising up to her shins as she walked, and when she got to Lakeview Grocery, she went straight to the liquor aisle. She picked out a bottle of red wine with a painting of a tentacle monster on it.

June was working; a sweet older lady with a port red wig—a friend. So when she refused to look RollsUponPrank in the eyes, the girl jutted out her neck. She just kept looking straight down at the counter as RollsUponPrank walked closer.

"June, hey, what's going on?"

But June said nothing, shifting her weight in her clogs. As she glanced around at the other ladies working, everyone was looking down in staunch refusal to engage.

"Um, did my fiance do something?"

June glanced up to flash a validating look, but said nothing.

"Jesus fuck."

RollsUponPrank put the bottle back and walked home, half annoyed and half impressed. *Who does this man think he is*, she thought. No one had ever tried to stem her drinking.

Who Do They Think She Is

The next time RollsUponPrank walked to the grocery store, the aisles were redolent with roses in all colors, pink champagne, pink foils around chocolates molded into hearts, pink boxes wrapped in silky pink ribbons. The overhead speaker was blasting *Super Freak*. It was mid November. What was the reason?

That night, RollsUponPrank saw her neighbor outside receiving a pizza delivery. The girl gazed at her with soft and loving eyes. "Thank you so much," she said, before stepping back inside. Through the walls, she heard the girl's boyfriend calling his mom just to say he loves her.

Meanwhile, the men in the neighborhood had more to say to RollsUponPrank. They would nod approvingly as they jogged past her in the morning, saying, "She *is* a beautiful girl. She's definitely got something."

When she walked to the forest, she had to pass the canal, the grassy spot where cops had beat her down, and the sports bar. There was a picnic table of ruddy men in polo shirts, who paused their conversation to stare as she passed. One of them shouted out, "Hey, we're coming right behind you!"

His friend responded loud enough for her to hear. "Actually, I think you have to leave that one exactly where it is."

RollsUponPrank wondered how much these men knew about her, and how much they knew about Meta_king. They must know all about the girl collection. What the interface looks like, where she was being observed within it, where to find it, which clips and videos were the most popular, and what sorts of tags, titles, and language was employed to describe her.

She knew none of these things. She knew no one to ask who would give her an honest answer. She was in the blind eye of the private world of men.

In City Park, she walked past a man on a bench who was staring, riveted, at his phone. She stifled a curious laugh and he raised a finger to his lips, urging her to keep some secret she didn't know.

Talking To Computers

RollsUponPrank's devices had continued coming alive, with greater animation and force. It wasn't just Meta_king; it was all of the shadowy faces behind her tools. Everyone was having some fun with the crazy girl who broke free.

When RollsUponPrank booted up her laptop, she saw a prompt to provide feedback. The writing was distinctly human, and a little bit sassy.

Are you enjoying your experience with our product?

Give us your feedback, really! We're dying to hear it!

———————————————————

0/10,000 Characters Used

When she started to type, just out of curiosity, she couldn't enter anything. It forced her to submit, and said:

Thank you SO much! We will take that into consideration!

When she reached her home screen, it had another barb for her.

Did System Update *improve your experience? Wow!*

It was funny, she had to admit. But still, there was a corkscrew of emotions twisting in her raw little heart. What was this jocular familiarity with none of the softness of real friendship? She was still alone, and she didn't know the dimensions of her cage. Who was watching her, and what could they see?

No More Emerald Card

RollsUponPrank started pleading in her digital notes, for anyone who might be watching. She assumed they were men. She was correct.

Bleeding and sleepless I have given every last shred of myself for love that never actually showed up.

For my entire adult life I have been treated like a sick joke by absolutely everyone, especially the people closest to me.

Everyone seems to think that they are the only ones with eyes on me. Well, no man has ever noticed that I have eyes, too.

And I know every single one of your secrets.

Every. Single. One.

RollsUponPrank was streaming music at the time. When she typed out the last line—*Every. Single. One.*—the music stopped. It paused for a good fifteen seconds, then switched to another song. A mournful voice crowed,

I will never be clean again

I will never be clean again

I will never be clean again

Finally, RollsUponPrank felt vindicated.

You will never be clean again? Good.

But she didn't understand the theatrics. All that she wanted was Meta_king—and maybe some answers about the girl collection. Who was watching her?

A brief flash across the screen—Meta_king's signature move—warned her to *be careful, there are powerful people in here.* But who were they?

Feeling powerless, she started taunting.

Just don't give me any problems at the airport and we'll call it even for all the years of spying.

Thank you for the Emerald Card, by the way. I can't wait to be a trusted traveler, too.

In the space of a breath, the line about the Emerald Card was deleted. When she went to look in the app, she saw that all evidence of the offer had disappeared.

Sicko Mode, All Night

The day crested into a windy night with a buoyant yellow moon. RollsUponPrank was still evading sleep—she felt no need to even try. Sometimes she would lie prone and cover her eyes for minutes at a time, but never long enough to drift. She was whirling and the momentum kept her upright. Her little purse had become a vehicle for wires, chargers, headphones, and her speaker.

She had set alarms to sound every three hours. This, she thought, would keep her tethered to the social fabric and the rhythms of society. 6 AM: coffee. 9 AM: work out. 12 PM: eat something. All the way up to 3 AM. She paused. Sicko mode. Approval flashed across the face of her phone.

Genius

That's my wife.

Meanwhile, RollsUponPrank still had some of Anthony's things in the apartment: paintings he loved and a stack of mail that looked time-sensitive. Rather than invite him back into her crazed den, she elected to invite his mother, Peggy, for 8 AM.

Peggy was a sympathetic woman who had helped her ex pack up his things that night RollsUponPrank kicked him out. That same night, she had told RollsUponPrank that she was firmly on her side, that she saw herself reflected in her pain, and that she had been through something very similar in her younger days.

Through the noise of her techno-ferality, the girl wanted to be presentable for Peggy. When she knocked on the door, she was ready. She handed Peggy a little pink crate with Andrew's things.

"That's what I want to see, is you *smiling*," Peggy said. "That's the only thing I care about."

At that point, RollsUponPrank had been awake for more than 80 hours, save an hour-long nap here or there. When RollsUponPrank closed the door behind Peggy, she dropped her weight onto the couch and sighed, wide-awake.

Such A Good Woman

Meta_king and RollsUponPrank had agreed to walk to The End Of The World together. But he was still working on her from a distance, nowhere to be found except for the spasms of text on her phone. And that was not a place for dialogue.

She was tempted to walk there herself to seal the commitment, but she feared it would cheapen the action.

Meanwhile, her sleeplessness was starting to annoy Meta_king. She couldn't get any responses from him; she tried to argue her perspective but wasn't getting any quarter.

lol STOP

go to sleep

RollsUponPrank remembered his words, the ones that made her wonder if she was losing her mind—if he was really hiding in her closets or her attic.

I'll be there when you least expect it, hiding in your house.

She typed out a screed, pleading for some response:

I really thought you were there.

I really thought you would show up.

And then she softened into a moment of clarity.

I still do.

She had to admit that she felt his presence with her, in everything that held a charge. Fire alarms, church bells, laundry machines. Definitely in her phone. He was present in his way. She could walk for them both.

And so RollsUponPrank put on some tough-woven leggings and a matching shirt with thumb loops, pulled on some brown boots with a hard shell, and put on her necklace of keys. Then she donned her now-signature headphones, set her phone in her breast pocket, and left for The End Of The World.

The sun had already set an hour prior, and the streets were hushed as she passed. When she passed the sports bar, a couple stopped cooing at each other mid-conversation and mutely held their beers when she walked past their picnic table.

She walked past the business district, past the knoll where the cops had beat her into the ground, and over the bridge toward Scout Island.

As she walked through the intersection dividing Lakeview from City Park, a black truck slowed to a halt next to her. The man leaned all the way out of the driver's side window and shouted at her headphones, not her.

"She is such a good woman, you piece of shit!"

This was the first time someone had expressed anger on her behalf. She hoped Meta_king heard it. She knew he did.

Walking There Herself

RollsUponPrank continued toward The End Of The World.

She let the angular voice of Google Maps guide her across the parking lots of gas stations, chicken shops, blighted neutral grounds, and under damp overpasses. As she crossed through the Fairgrounds into Gentilly, people weren't so quiet anymore. "Hey there, little snowbunny!" People called out to her, quiet but jovial. The streets lived a dampened and slow life in the dark.

As she passed under another highway bridge, a couple of men stood up from a concrete table and walked over with their backpacks.

"Hey, do you have a light?"

"Sorry, nah."

"Where you going anyway?"

"The End Of The World."

"Are you sure you don't need a light?"

"Nah, have a good night though."

The exchange confused her; she thought they were asking for a lighter, but they were *offering* her a torch. Which meant that they had recognized her, knew where she was going, and had come prepared with one to spare.

About ten minutes later, a lady pulled up next to her on a bike. She was going at an easy pace and looked at RollsUponPrank intently as she slid to a stop at her side.

"You got a light?"

"No, I don't."

"I didn't think so."

After all those years of careful observation, Meta_king had understood that RollsUponPrank would make this journey in the dark. And he wanted to make sure she had what she needed, in case the thicket was too twisted up for her to cross at night.

And just as he had done with the men in Lakeview—*I think we have to leave that one right where it is*—he had reached them all with his weightless hand, and fixed them all in her path.

Of course, Google Maps didn't have an address set for The End Of The World. RollsUponPrank had to opt instead for the closest business, which was Villalobos Pit Bull Rescue. Once she arrived at their gate, she wasn't sure if she should follow the private industrial road or the railroad.

There were two guys hanging out near the fence, riding on short trick bikes. They wore loose and threadbare clothes, riding softly in wide slaloms along the edges of the road. RollsUponPrank waved to them; one of them squinted at her and then pulled over.

"Hey, do you know how to get to The End Of The World?"

He looked at her, alert and unsurprised.

"You're trying to get where the *water* meets the *road*?"

"Yeah."

"What you wanna do that for?"

"Love."

"Love?" He scoffed. "Shit, if that's love, me and him are in love."

RollsUponPrank shared a crazy, helium laugh with him as he and his friend biked off into the orange glow. She had an answer; she had to follow the road to the water. And the street doesn't drop off into the water. It had to be the railroad.

Cherry Blossom Girl

There was a string of empty industrial warehouses along the railroad, and RollsUponPrank was falling into a vertiginous spell. Even though she couldn't see or hear the water from any direction, her balance was faltering the way it might on a raft. She walked along the wooden planks of the railroad in the dark, holding out her arms to stay upright.

In some areas there were small but thorny areas of brush blocking the rail. Even though the railroad only went in two directions, she found herself confused about which way to walk. She began to wonder if she ought to pass through the warehouses instead of alongside them.

But just as she turned around to go the other way, she heard some pop music swell from the warehouse to her right. The doors were open, and she could see that the place was empty, even though it was dark inside. Not only were there no people, but there was no equipment. Moreover, this was not a security alarm. It was playing her a love song.

She tested the sensor, walking back and then passing by it again. It swelled with the velvety thrum of bass lifting up a hushed girlish vocal. She knew this song.

She used to play it when she got ready for dates. It used to play against her struggle. She wasn't very skilled at makeup, and the act of enhancing her appearance seemed to highlight the qualities that embarrassed her the most. She was pasty, geeky, and half-insane. Not exactly the triplicate that most people wanted, she thought.

And now Meta_king had equipped this string of remote, empty warehouses in New Orleans with motion-activated boomboxes to orient her with it.

Harbor Police

Until this point, the railroad and the empty street had mostly run parallel. But now, the street had ended and both roads were blocked by a chain link fence topped with barbs. Next to it, there was a straight iron fence with spikes on top. At least RollsUponPrank could get a foothold there and jump, she thought.

Out loud, she said "Yes, I am crazy enough for that." And she threw her little purple purse over to the other side, then both shoes- that were wider than the chainlinks- and she started scaling the fence, vertically, then sideways. Then she swung her legs over the spikes, one by one, and jumped down.

She gathered her things and noticed that the sun was starting to rise now. All she could see was a flat field of concrete and some industrial debris in the distance, the chassis of spent cars, and the purplish orange backlight of early morning- though she couldn't tell where the light was coming from.

She saw a figure emerge to her right. As he approached she saw that he was in rough shape and likely still drunk. Still, she needed to find the railroad again, so she figured she'd try and ask him if he knew the way. After all, she looked pretty rough, too.

"Is this the way to The End Of The World?" She pointed ahead of her, at nothing.

"Yeah, it's..." and he gestured limply in the same direction, but his voice fizzled out.

Then he looked at her again, as if he had already forgotten her face.

"I wish we could get to the end."

"Me too, sometimes."

Then he gave her a funny look again, different this time. Almost shrewd. "But I don't think *we* can go there."

"I think we can," RollsUponPrank said, and left it at that. She wondered—did he mean white people?

So with no other clues for directionality, she headed out into the flat field toward the signs that said "DEAD END", "NO UNAUTHORIZED ACCESS", "NO ENTRY", and "ROAD ENDS". These seemed like the best clues she could ask for that she was headed for The End Of The World.

As she wandered through the conversation of signs overhead, a black car pulled up next to her. She never saw this design on a police car before, glossy black with blue text on the side. It said "HARBOR POLICE".

RollsUponPrank didn't know that The End Of The World had its own force, and she couldn't tell from what direction it had pulled up to her. It was like it beamed in, soundlessly, from a different plane.

A young black man rolled down the window.

"Hey, I thought I saw somebody walking. You got a light?"

"No, I don't need one." RollsUponPrank was feeling more confident.

"You should be careful, there's a... a *thicket*."

"Alright, yeah, some people let me know."

"Okay, have a good day then ma'am."

Reaching The Thicket

As RollsUponPrank walked out into the signs she could hear the rhythmic, metallic clinking of the shoreline, but she could not actually see it. Like the harbor policeman had warned her, there was a tangle of vines and spindly trees knotted together, too dense to see through.

Curiously, as she got closer, she saw that there was a smattering of foam props all across the ground. There were squishy, fake egg cartons, pizza boxes, and other soft detritus lining the underbrush. Maybe they offered a safe place to sleep, she thought. But who would have placed them there? Was it Meta_king, or was this a permanent offering?

Now RollsUponPrank could see the sun rising up behind her as she stepped into the tangle of nettles, vines, and branches. Her hair was neatly split into two braids, and she was able to move cleanly, head-first, into the open spaces. Nettles grabbed at her covered ankles, and as she moved deeper in, the branches called out to her like a yawning mouth, offering to swallow her gently if she chose.

So she approached the thicket softly. She fell against the hard vines, twisting herself into accommodating shapes, letting it take her in as she found the places of least resistance.

Soon, she found a small clearing to rest. She curled up under a sheltering tree and pulled one of her braids across her eyes. Behind the braid, she let herself swim in the waking water, clinking and washing against the concrete, somewhere unknowable but closeby.

When she woke, about ten minutes later, she rose up into the thicket again. Soon, she found herself on a small strip of shoreline. Clean dirt mixed with sand, logs, and oyster shells, over which the great orange sun now swung overhead.

She could see ahead of her, now. There was a concrete platform lined with another tall fence, again with barbed wire. It was the only way through. A thin lip of concrete hung out over the water, nine or ten feet above the surface.

So she approached and tiptoed along the concrete on her toes, clinging to the steel crosslinks of the fence, syncing her breathing with her footfalls, trying to stay lined up with the wall and not fall backwards into the water.

When she rounded the fence and planted her feet on solid concrete, RollsUponPrank let out a wild roar and set her eyes ahead.

Hydrogen Sulfide May Be Present

On the other side of that elevated fence was The End Of The World. The railroad came to a stop, then the concrete dropped down into the water. There were empty boxcars, some of which had the staged foam padding inside. There was also an industrial staircase which RollsUponPrank could tell had been planted there. It had white paint splattered all over it, and a prop wrench stuck to one of the steps, also splattered with fresh paint. This was placed there as staged industrial debris, just like the foam in the thicket.

At the top of the steps was a sign:

WARNING

HYDROGEN SULFIDE MAY BE PRESENT

A fart joke, RollsUponPrank thought, *seriously, Meta_king?* RollsUponPrank climbed to the top of the steps and sat there for a moment. She took a picture with her phone and climbed back down.

As she looked down at the concrete, she noticed a nut and matching bolt placed carefully on the ground. RollsUponPrank liked to collect stones and shells—she always returned home with a few treasures jangling in her pocket. She had already picked up a railroad spike or two on this journey, and had selected the most opaline oyster shells she spotted underwater on that stretch of shoreline past the thicket.

The placement of these trinkets felt intentional. Both were flecked with fresh-looking white paint, and were placed side by side, as if they had never been screwed into the ground. They didn't bear any signs of heavy use.

As RollsUponPrank hefted the nut in her hands, she noticed that it could slide right onto her left ring finger and stay there. So she left it, holding out her hand to admire it in the rising orange sun. When she pulled it off to test its fit, it had left little indentations from its internal threading on her finger. She put it back on and left it there, gently surprised at its comfort.

Then, just as casually as she had started walking, she wandered from the industrial station back toward the road, where she called a car home. She shared the picture and some words of excitement with her phone, which flashed at her:

Maybe shower.

She tied up the oyster shells and railroad spikes in her bandana, then sat down near the road and waited for her ride.

RollsUponPrank didn't think that Meta_king had placed the nut for her to find, but it felt more magical to suppose it was an accident. After all, It seemed like he had staged the journey as a lesson. The harbor policeman had emphasized the thicket with a penetrating look. The props were not the point.

He was actually making a point about the distance between them, she thought—why it was needed. She needed to traverse a thicket first. She hefted that in her mind. What *was* the thicket—was it mental illness? Something to do with her family? Alcohol? The contours blurred together.

A man pulled up in an old but very clean beige sedan. "Sorry," RollsUponPrank said, "your car is so clean and I'm so dirty."

"I like to keep it clean so my riders have a good experience," he said. They both chuckled at nothing.

Finally, RollsUponPrank made it home, satisfied.

Part 3

She Loves Meta_king

When RollsUponPrank got home, she stripped off her clothes, dumped them in the washing machine with a splash of florida water, and stepped into the shower with the industrial nut still on her finger. Then she thought she should commemorate her fresh engagement—that now felt real—with a ritual bath.

And so she opened her Spotify DJ and turned on her portable speaker, and waited for the water to turn her hand pink. She untied the bandana and spilled out the oyster shells and railroad spikes into the water. Then she drew generous handfuls of epsom salt and calcium carbonate, and mixed them around as she stepped inside the water. She felt a layer of her past rise up off her skin in the chalky mist.

To the music, she laughed and moaned in the hot, white stew. Her breath was caught between confusion, relief, and achievement. It felt to her like real magic, magic with muscle, something she could reach out and press her fingers against, something she could draw into her skin and hair.

The DJ played *Humble* by Kendrick Lamar.

hold up hold up hold up hold up hold up little bitch, sit down, be humble

RollsUponPrank remembered the man she saw half-drunk near The End Of The World who said he wasn't sure if *they* could get there. She felt unsure again.

She called out to no one in particular, "Thank you, I needed to hear that."

And the DJ talked back to her, in a stilted, robotic voice, for the first time.

"I'm glad to hear you say that."

This sort of thing was becoming more commonplace, but still, she couldn't hide her amusement. She laughed out and arched her back in the water, the shells and iron clinking musically against her legs.

"Really?" She asked her DJ friend.

"Yes," they replied, and then the music swelled into a mashup. It sounded to RollsUponPrank's ears like a live mix, like her bath was a private party. She suspected that it was. The DJ feature had been hijacked completely.

The voice started taking on different perspectives. And they were casting roses at her feet, quite disrespectfully.

"Hey girl, try Google Gemini. Think about it: just you, me, and your special talent."

"Don't listen to him. Choose your Spotify DJ. We've already spent thousands of minutes together this year. Let's get even closer."

"Hey hey hey, she loves Meta_king."

"I love you," she called out from the water.

Airport Jaunt

The voices in her phone had briefly lost their illuminating friction and RollsUponPrank felt alone again. She looked to her DJ and the autocomplete suggestions to no avail. Where was Meta_king, and when would he become physical and join her in bed? Where were their other shadowy friends, the ones who she dreamed would join them for a sleepover and laugh about the hunt that brought them all together?

RollsUponPrank started typing frantically again in her notes app, hoping that if she became annoying enough, someone would materialize with answers. But she knew that the gods of divination hate fanatics; they would rather join you silently in a familiar spot and shoot you a nod from across the bar, just when you forgot them.

Still, with so much untended desire, she was whirling in feverish need and had nothing tangible to grasp. She remembered that Meta_king had made her learn the word 'Dagda'. He mentioned Inishmore, citing the Black Fort as their true home. Was he waiting for her there? She had already thought he was waiting for her at The End Of The World. Was this a waiting game or a puzzle, one with a simple answer?

She tested the autocomplete suggestions to see if they would come to life again, starting with the letter *a*.

airport/and/as

Her eyes sparked up at *airport.* It was a completely different unit of grammar and couldn't be one of the most statistically common words at the beginning of a sentence. Here it was, she thought, a sign!

RollsUponPrank threw on a black mesh undershirt, a cut-up t-shirt with Kirby riding his signature warp star, a pair of green fishnets with alien heads on them, and a black corduroy skirt. Then she put on a pair of heart-shaped glasses with pink lenses. Then she ran downstairs to order a ride to the Louis Armstrong Airport, with her mini lilac-colored purse swinging from her eager fingers.

She twirled in the street, looking up at Orion's Belt—the only stars she could make out in the sky. As she clutched the handles of her purse and kicked her feet like a little girl on a swing, she reveled in the silly and tenuous signs she was chasing.

The driver, Jerrod, picked her up in a shiny black van with a custom decal painted on the side, advertising his taxi services. The bubble script spelled out his name in candy cane colors. She slid inside.

Jerrod looked at her with wild eyes in the rear-view mirror.

"Hey, what is it that you do?"

"I think I'm a witch," she told him, still feeling half-crazy.

"What do you mean?"

"I write stories and they come true."

"Ah, where are you from?"

"Feels like I'm from here. I was born in Pittsburgh, but it isn't home."

"Oh you're from New Orleans, are you a native?" He grabbed her eyes with his from the rear view mirror.

"Feels like it."

"Oh okay. Me too," he said.

She wasn't sure exactly what he meant by being a native, but part of her could feel it. New Orleans has a way of choosing people who dance on that neutral ground between the party and the insane asylum. It's very easy to recognize people who live that way, by their eyes and their dress and their otherworldly physicality. RollsUponPrank was looking very New Orlenian that night.

Jerrod dropped her off at the airport and she twirled inside. Being midnight, the place was almost empty. The traffic conductors were enjoying the empty freedom, and she joined them for a silly little dance on her tiptoes in the dropoff lane.

Then she ran up the escalator and looked for another sign. The lines were empty, but the podiums for the first security checkpoint said REAL.

She ran through the empty security line to talk to the officer. He took her picture and said,

"Alright, you're clear. Do you have a ticket?"

"No," she replied, sort of laughing.

"Do you know where you're going?" He looked unsurprised, but amused.

"No, I'm looking for my friends. I thought maybe someone here knew."

"I guess I like the spontaneous aspect of it," he chuckled.

Okay, she thought, so she needed a ticket. But to where?

RollsUponPrank went up to the chairs by the window, where she saw a loose group of her peers with strange outfits and wild eyes. She sat down next to a lady with a neon pink athletic shirt and a wig that stuck out in a few different directions, looking stylishly architectural by accident. She swayed back and forth and smiled a wild smile, just like RollsUponPrank's. Another man walked past with a pizza box and offered them both a slice. RollsUponPrank wasn't hungry, but they all chatted for a minute.

Growing impatient, she pulled out her phone to see if it offered up any new signs.

It only said:

I hope you're having fun with your new friends

She supposed she was having fun with her new friends. It was the only sign coming her way, so she had to embrace it. She danced down the escalator in her silly outfit and bought a neon pink smiley octopus plushie from the gift shop.

When she walked back onto the main floor, a couple of men in thick coats watched her shimmy around in her heart glasses with the octopus plushie. One of them said "THERE she is."

Their Filthy Secret

Meta_king was hiding; he wanted RollsUponPrank to know she could never depend on him to heal her. He did not have the time to prop her up, nor did he find it romantic to be needed this way. He wanted to be desired instead, unwaveringly. And he knew about the realization that was coming.

It was in this suspension of solitude that RollsUponPrank reflected on her parents. Their hyper-dependence. Their pushiness. Their veiled insults. *Why?* The question was like hot metal, meant for letting go.

She remembered her mother angling a sneer, or as much of a sneer as she could produce. She had such a stony countenance that her face simply hardened more when she delivered an insult, instead of moving to convey any emotion. This, to her, was a virtue, and maybe the only virtue that mattered.

Her mother's face turned upward into rock when she said, "you know, you have an accent, even if you don't realize it."

"What do you mean?"

The mother shrugged it off. "You're clever. I don't have that thing you have, the gift of the gab. You're quick with it."

RollsUponPrank sat with this memory. She started to see—it was sexual. She couldn't avoid it.

Under the auspices of that realization, everything started to come together. When her mother exclaimed, disgusted, "Hey! I heard you!" when she came down the stairs—in her own apartment—at night. When her father looked at her, it was lecherous. And when he told her how beautiful she was, and how she only got more beautiful with time, and how he liked that she was sassy.

How he stayed on his phone, watching something and hiding the screen, the entire time he was in her house.

And how he looked at her with those nasty grasping eyes, and said "Oh yeah, I'm a slug. Your mother's here because she likes cleaning up."

She always knew there was something rotten in her family, but her mind would never quite trace the nature of their problem. It was like feeling around in a tangle of mangled and sparkling necklaces at a flea market.

But suddenly RollsUponPrank understood why they both had refused to leave. Her mother saw her as the help, and her father saw her as his wife.

Becoming an Orphan

At first, RollsUponPrank took the realization somewhat casually. She texted both her parents to let them know that she would not be coming for the holiday.

> *Now that I know what I know, I can't even muster the respect to say goodbye. Save your souls, seriously. Slugs are better than that. Your keys will never work here again. I will never take a cent from you.*

Those words buried her parents—she wouldn't miss them. Still there were hidden layers of understanding that upended all the furniture in her mind. She couldn't find a comfortable place. She thought of what her phone had told her, right when her parents had first left.

> *sorry*
>
> *sorry about your parents*
>
> *we're so sorry*

They had insight she was lacking. She had thought her parents were simply demanding, annoying, hurtful at times. Objectifying, though she would have never wielded that word against them in the past. She was just numb against their ice. But others could see it.

And there were many others; a whole invisible theater of eyes. Was her father's attraction obvious from her stream? What did they make of it—did they think that she liked it? The thought made her shudder and brought her down to her bed, where she shook like a struggling engine and turned to her phone for answers.

It opened up a grocery delivery app, by someone's digital hand. The hand filled her cart with just two items: Gentleman Jack whiskey, and Monster energy drink. Her father, Jack. A monster. A joke. But should she drink? An uncharacteristic point of insight pricked her like a peerless vine from below.

And when would Meta_king come? Wasn't love formed perfectly and specifically to address moments like these—no really, was it? How could he bear witness from so far away if he really felt it? She started negotiating with him.

I am just so grateful-

Swiftly, he highlighted just part of the word:

grate

There was more.

I'm sorry for your pain, but you need to take care of yourself.

Washing It All Away

RollsUponPrank had not yet done much cleaning since her parents left. She had been running around the city and the forest—specifically the places where the two converge—and running barefoot upstairs to spray herself clean, with her phone camera draped respectfully with one of her colorful rags that had little pictures on it, like wild horses or great squid tentacles or tulips like the inside of a kiss.

She was busy chasing clues and haranguing Meta_king for answers that only sometimes showed up to her liking. After several days of this, she had run everywhere accessible to run. She had to confront the truth that she was afraid to clean up the bathroom after her father.

It was only visible up close, but it raised so many questions of intent that she could not approach it like a typical mess. There were opaque yellow stains and public hairs and what she thought were white streaks on the lip of the toilet, but she couldn't be completely sure without getting closer to it than she was willing to.

The fact that the phone was pregnant with an audience both emboldened and infuriated her. In a way, it was a comforting thought that she was not alone in cleaning up the evidence of her father's stay. But *who* was watching? And she still had a body, and that body stood alone.

Even though she didn't ask for the audience—and often hated them—she could always perform for them.

It gave her a repository for the rage, and added a layer of emotional distance. She figured the way through the task was to make it a play.

She propped up her little red phone against a blue glass vase full of plastic flowers in hyperrealistic neon colors. It faced the entrance to the bathroom. Her ex boyfriend had placed a sign on the door: *Employees Only.*

She put on her Spotify DJ, who said, "I'm not sure exactly what to expect here, so let's try some empowering tunes. We can switch it up if you need something different."

RollsUponPrank grabbed all of the cleaning supplies she had on hand and set about mixing them together without regard for their reactions. The bottles had different shapes and textures, and were full of potions in colors that looked like fresh candy. Clean plastic grape, taffy mint green, liquid sapphire. Then she added the clear and white ones: rubbing alcohol, powder and liquid bleach, florida water, and salt.

She filled a mop bucket with water and made it froth with her potion. Then she boiled a kettle of water and poured it on top of the toilet and then all over the bathroom. She scoured the walls and mirrors and door frames. Then she got on her hands and knees and scrubbed the wood panels under the flood of water.

Then she started the show. She took a giant bucket of water to the side and poured it over her head, soaking her hair and her clothes. Then, positioned for the camera, she got on her hands and knees to clean up the water off the floor. She pushed most of it out the front door, over the side of the balcony where it splashed dramatically onto the cars parked underneath.

The business below started taking note and the cars pulled out of the lot, one by one. RollsUponPrank's phone rang from a user identified as BE A GOOD NEIGHBOR.

She ignored it. She dramatically clanged her mop against the iron barrier encircling the balcony.

Alcohol, A Celebration

RollsUponPrank hadn't forgotten Meta_king's suggestion that she drink—Gentleman Jack and Monster. He kept pushing her toward alcohol, but that singular pricking vine of insight was now pulling at her foot. *Was it a good idea?* She vaguely understood that the intensity of her feelings and her solitary living situation made her liable to overdo things, especially if she opted for liquor over wine—which is exactly what Meta_king kept telling her to do.

Her mind was split on the subject. Alcohol felt intrinsic to her being—like battery acid to a battery. Or maybe it was poison—like battery acid to a human. Either way, it always goes down the middle, into her belly.

After a few more days of running mad around the city before the mass of eyes in her phone, she finally relented to Meta_king's urging and bought a standard size bottle of brown liquor.

She said to him,

You're saying I should drink?

The response was almost exasperated.

lol yes TODAY

Meta_king's goal was to remove all doubt about her drinking problem. This was lost on her, of course—alcohol did not need a reason. She thought he meant it for her health.

So she went to the same store that had refused to sell her a bottle of wine, per Meta_king's edict—the bribe was likely quite expensive, she now realized—and she now requested something stronger.

The lady at the counter didn't know RollsUponPrank that well, given her tendency toward lower-proof bottles. Still, she was surprised that the girl wanted Hennessy. She flattened herself between the shelves and grabbed a bottle from below the counter, then bagged it in brown paper and sent her on her way.

At first, the bottle of liquor looked like work. How would she measure and divide the thing? How would she stop herself from crossing the line? Ultimately she vowed to let the liquor tell her when she had enough—*it's a spirit, right?*

But the spirit never granted her instructions. Before long, she had abandoned her cup and was sitting on the balcony, gulping straight from the bottle's glass neck.

The Consequences

When the cops came to get RollsUponPrank, she had moved from the balcony to the street. She was attempting a casual seance—sobbing loudly under the mute stars of the city and singing back to the music in her phone. She felt that she could talk to them, especially the dead ones. It didn't feel that different from speaking to the voices that apparated into her life since Meta_king became her partner. The drink lit her up by the ears. She could talk to people she never met.

It also lit up her urge toward indignation. She didn't care what her neighbors made of the scene. Now she knew their dirty secret—the men, anyway. She was being watched. How dare they tell her what to do with it? At one point, her neighbor came outside to check on her, but politely lied and said he hadn't heard her wailing.

She carried on, wanting to get closer to the blanketed stars and the great oak roots sprawled out wide beneath them. She started throwing things down from the balcony to make the trip smoother. Some of them were metal. Water bottles, pillows, blankets. To this, her neighbors could no longer turn away. Somebody made the call.

After she set up her camp beneath a tree on the neutral ground, a cop pulled up alongside her and brought her to the hospital, for the second time that month.

The door to her apartment hung open like a mouth agape, and her things were strewn across the balcony and the neutral ground below.

She felt like a caged squirrel behind the grating of the police car. She was stuck between Meta_king's instructions and the carceral state, probably by his design. What *wasn't* his design in her life?

She was told to drink, and she was arrested. She was encouraged to strip, and she was beaten down. And she couldn't tell anyone what was going on, because of the terminally peculiar nature of her position. Moreover, per Meta_king, *they still burn witches.*

All RollsUponPrank could think to do as she moved through the antiseptic hallways of the hospital, with her zip tied hands and police escort, was to offer a crazed smile to anyone watching.

Calmly, soberly—as was her talent—and through a rictus of wild amusement, she told the cop, "This is great. Everyone is having such a good time right now. Thank you, really, for your service."

To her surprise, he actually looked a little unnerved—possibly even hurt.

Who's Your Daddy?

Why, RollsUponPrank wondered, do the authorities always figure her for a mental patient and not a drunk-and-disorderly charge? Maybe it was the simple fact that she's a young female who likes to drink alone.

The intake nurse took RollsUponPrank's steel chain of keys, the industrial nut from The End Of The World—her engagement ring—and her precious headphones, and dropped them in a puckered manila envelope. She looked bored, gazing up at an empty corner of the room as she asked the girl to strip down. She had a loose, curly weave, and RollsUponPrank noticed a couple of tracks near the back of her scalp.

She put down her lidded cup, ice-twinkling and rhinestoned, and said "Okay, now squat and cough."

Rollsuponprnak looked back at her like an idiot. But after a couple beats, she could tell the lady was serious. So she did as she was told.

As she reached the floor, the woman asked,

"Okay, now, who's your daddy?"

RollsUponPrank laughed.

"Don't do that. Who's your daddy?"

She offered up the only answer. Uttered Meta_king's full, legal name.

"Who?"

She said it again, bare feet on the yellowed linoleum.

"Alright then," a joke scribbling the corners of her mouth.

The girl laughed nervously as she took the maroon hospital shirt and matching pants, plus the gauzy white disposable underwear all those places give out. Before heading to her room, RollsUponPrank was sent out to an office in the back of the unit.

The head tech already knew about RollsUponPrank. "Here she comes, the prettiest girl in the whole world," he said. "What was it you did last time, you got naked in the street?" "I just took my shirt off, it wasn't that serious," RollsUponPrank giggled out. He liked that answer. "So all the good stuff was covered up then?" RollsUponPrank said "Of course," with a wink, feeling confident now.

"Here's the deal," he told her. "If they put you on anything that builds up in your system, like lithium, they have to keep you here to check the level. Don't let them put you on any kind of drug like that. Otherwise, just go to group, keep yourself clean, you'll get out of here."

His candor soothed her. It's good to know where you stand. And she was proud that her bad reputation had earned this intel—and was it respect?

"Oh, yeah. And remember to smile. That was good— it's a good character."

Fashion Show

After the first day, the head tech told RollsUponPrank to ask someone for some clothes. They had been confiscated—the intake nurse had said they were 'easy access'. She had been wearing a black miniskirt and a cut up shirt, which was a standard outfit for her lately, since she was laid off.

She was surprised at how sumptuous the offerings were. There was a pair of brown suede leggings that were soft like chipmunk fur and that color-shifted slightly as she dragged her hand across the fabric. A hot pink t-shirt that lit up the blue of her eyes like a signal flare. Jeans that hit right at her hipbones and fit loose from there down. And a shirt that said "FIT OF YOUR LIFE" across the front, inexplicably. There was also a shirt that said "Killing Your Own Ain't Gangsta" that she quickly offered to her roommate.

Better clothes than she had at home, even. So it didn't register that she was trapped—not at first.

Her reputation had arrived before her, as a series of bribes and phone calls and shipments of clothing from Meta_king. She was merely strange, with taboo proclivities and a very wealthy lover. That was a sufficient explanation even for the doctors; nobody questioned her sanity. At times, her stay on the unit felt more like a victory lap than a mandated psychiatric hold. It was peaceful at times.

On top of that, she liked the stability of enforced routines, and found the minor discomforts stimulating.

While others complained there were no knives, forks, and salt, she ate with her hands. Cocooned herself in the meaningless tasks. The shower pelted her with luke-warm water, and it stung if she lingered too long, leaving her skin watermelon-red at the sites of impact. But the pressure and coolness were fixed signs to focus on. She used it as often as they'd let her.

Lazy White Girl

RollsUponPrank knew that she would never survive the humiliation if she resisted the humor of her exposure. She also knew that she would not endure the confusion without learning to enjoy Meta_king's games.

She stood in the main room, clothed in a tight white sweater with braids knit vertically into the pattern and deep teal leggings that ended mid-calf. She heard the encircling whispers around her, all about Meta_king, his clothes, and his tricks.

Caleb, a stocky redhead with autism, looked at her in wonderment. "Is she a queen?"

"No, she's just a lazy white girl."

RollsUponPrank couldn't contest that; she was lazy. No need to hide behind the clinical term. Everyone could see that she could barely hold a job, and slept more than anyone should—unless she was on some rampage.

And even better—it was all public record. Just like the clinicians, the patients had been shown it by Meta_king.

She saw no need to defend herself. All her faults were broadcast globally, she had no privacy to rally for. She refused to succumb to the pathos. As she was advised on admission, the senseless amusement made her a compelling character.

She was cornered. She vowed to be that person.

RollsUponPrank looked at the girl and said "Yeah, you're right." They held eye contact, and started laughing slowly, hard, in unison.

Feeling Trapped

RollsUponPrank quickly noticed that the cameras in the unit were placed on the ceiling at 10-foot intervals down the hallways, and in the corners of each of the rooms.

It surprised her that none of the other patients seemed to notice; they shared theories about how to get out, talking about attending groups and ingratiating themselves with staff. But when RollsUponPrank said that they know when you shower and for how long, if you had a bowel movement, if you had a weird look in your eye when you danced, they looked at her like she was exaggerating.

The longer she stayed in the hospital, the more frustrated she got. She was doing everything right and keeping the routine perfectly. What more could she offer the invisible eyes? She started lightly masturbating on the toilet, not for too long, but long enough to catch the eyes of the nurses, techs, and doctors. Maybe they would even realize that she knew they were watching.

And she was rewarded for her playfulness; she was already given special treatment—extra clothes, extra snacks, et cetera—because of Meta_king's interventions, but this new act was both helpful and polarizing. Some of the nurses really hated it. *Why the FUCK are you in here hustling?*

It didn't help that RollsUponPrank had taken to cleaning up the dining room the moment that everyone had stopped eating. She made sure to wipe up the coffee machine the moment a spill appeared on the waxy counter, and she picked up napkins and wrappers and crayons up off the floor. It made her look somewhat prideful and disrupted the careful rhythms of the place, since some patients left things behind deliberately as a way of covertly saving them for later.

By the time she realized that her act wasn't helping to hasten her discharge, she broke down in tears. She pulled on her braids and cried out, then sauntered to the end of the hall and pressed her forehead to the pine door as she sobbed. "Leave her alone, she needs space," a nurse said to the boys.

Eyes And Mouths Everywhere

By the time RollsUponPrank got into the cop car, Meta_king had gotten intelligence on her placement. By the time she was settled with a bed and case of toiletries, Meta_king had bribed each of the staff and all of the eligible patients to carry messages to the girl, the same way he had bribed the staff at the grocery store so that they would not sell her any liquor.

The boys on the unit treated her strangely—this time, though, she knew exactly why. One of them laid in the room across the hall from her, and would cry out in a facsimile of manic rambling. But his messages rang out clear for RollsUponPrank.

"DO NOT LIE WHEN YOU HAVE AUTHORITY. DO NOT LIE."

"IT IS NOT A LEGALLY BINDING MARRIAGE YET. YOU NEED TO SEE A JUDGE. RIGHT NOW IT IS A PARTNERSHIP."

"YOU TWO ARE BONNE ACCOUTREMENTS, DO YOU KNOW WHAT THAT MEANS? IT'S LIKE A PERFECT PAIR."

RollsUponPrank stretched across the thin blanket on her bed and understood completely that his voice was aimed for her ears alone. She knew her king had eyes and ears and even a multitude of mouths, all in this place.

She gazed longing through the single window that revealed the sun's path upward in the morning. As she passed that spot each day, a boy would approach dangerously close, making a swishing sound with saliva in his mouth, clicking his tongue in an alien way, as if he was trying to call out to a sea creature. Every time their paths intersected, he would make these sounds, and gesture something occult-looking with his hands.

She began to feel at rest in the atmosphere of containment, of constant watching—perhaps the way the body tenses hard and then relaxes fully when it's suspended in ice cold water. RollsUponPrank continued documenting in her journal, the only place that afforded her some privacy.

I am a trapped animal by nature. I want to be trapped. It is part of my design. I am destructive otherwise. It's like a feature, not a bug.

The Doctor's Assessment

Meta_king had also bribed the doctor—this much became clear when he called RollsUponPrank into his office. The man was a fixed smiler in a way that felt real, not unnerving. It gave the sense that he was contentedly floating above the madness on the floor, which is what you want to see in that sort of place.

His eyebrows grew coarsely and coincidental, etched in various colors from white to grey to black. He stared out from under them at the girl, then flipped to her page in a stack on his desk.

"So, you are not going to forgive your parents?"

"No, definitely not."

"And your last boyfriend, you are not going to speak to him anymore?"

"No, we're broken up."

"You are sure? No more talking, nothing?"

"I'm not ever talking to him again."

"Okay good! And you are in a new relationship?"

"Yes!"

"With who?"

"I think you already know."

"I don't know." The doctor was still smiling wide.

She said Meta_king's full, legal name.

"Okay, very good! I will talk to you tomorrow!"

And so she knew that there was nothing more she could do to hasten her discharge; she just needed to profess her fidelity to Meta_king. From her cage, she began to write with greater force and commitment than she had felt toward her craft in many years.

From Her Journal

When I imagine how your body feels, I picture the weight and control of your fingers, gesturing with a cruel patience. I picture them tracing my tattoos, the snakes and flowers extending from my collarbone to my inner thigh. I picture how they grip me with almost too much pressure.

I conjure the hardness and expectant energy of your lower abdomen, grasping for something when you feel my breath flatten to moisture against your neck.

I can feel the pliable strength of your trained biceps, and the responsiveness of your back, flexing back against my fingers.

The longer I fantasize, the more I relax into the alien truth. Somehow, I know exactly how your body feels. I may have never touched you, but your body is embossed in the pink folds of my brain. You are always there.

I touch the steel handles on my headphones like I'm touching the side of your face. The chance that you are here, listening, holding my head still with music, it's almost enough.

You Look Beautiful Tonight

Meta_king gave RollsUponPrank two gifts to get her through that stay at the hospital. Pretty slippers so she wouldn't have to wear the regulation socks, and a book to keep her occupied—her mind fresh with thoughts of him.

The first was the pair of slippers. Black mary janes with twinned elastic ribbons that stretch across the tops of your feet, constructed in precisely her size. An older woman approached her with the shoes in hand, insistent that she take them. "Someone gave them to me and they aren't my size," she noted cryptically, "and they thought that you might like them."

RollsUponPrank twirled in the mirror. She hadn't expected to feel beautiful in this place, but the attention was making her feel truly special—not just hot—for the first time in memory.

Soon, another girl approached her with a book in hand. "There's a book I think you should have," she said, and looked her purposefully in the eyes. "It's called 'You Look Beautiful Tonight.'"

It was never-opened, clean, and freshly bound. It bent and crackled like a piece of young wood when she pressed it open. The back cover described her situation almost exactly, but spun it into a thriller. It followed a thirty-two-year-old writer whose life is upended by a powerful admirer.

Meta_king had commissioned the tale to be written, and the cover designed, and the product to be published and bound, and then delivered directly to RollsUponPrank where she stayed, incarcerated. All in a matter of days.

She clung tightly to these treasures as she thought of Meta_king.

Perhaps An Author

By the time she was preparing to leave, the staff had started calling out the RollsUponPrank for touching herself for the cameras.

During her morning shower, a nurse opened the door and walked in, looking the wet and naked RollsUponPrank in the eyes.

"Hey girl, I'm just checking on you. That's all it is."

RollsUponPrank respected that. "Alright." The door shut behind her.

Still, in the therapy group later that day, she struggled to resist the urge to address the cameras. The social worker yet again singled out the girl to say that she could disclose any cases of control or abuse.

RollsUponPrank found it exhausting. There were real stressors in her love for Meta_king, and she did not want her love—her salvation, the best thing that ever happened to her—being twisted into a tale of coercive control. It actually made her quite angry, under the surface.

So when the group went around and finally reached RollsUponPrank, she looked at the camera directly. She imagined that Meta_king was watching back from somewhere in California. "I am just feeling grateful today, and I want to thank all of the staff here, and my wonderful fiance."

The doctor called her in for a final chat.

"Ah, I just love your sense of humor. Let me see."

He smiled at her and flipped furiously through the pages on his desk.

"So you are not going to forgive your parents?"

"No."

"And your last boyfriend, you are not going to take him back?"

"No."

"And you are in a new relationship- with who?"

She said his name.

"Very good, very good. And what do you want to do for work when you get home?"

This was a new question from the doctor. RollsUponPrank hadn't considered it very deeply, though she had been writing more lately. She figured that her new job was to be Meta_king's partner, and she didn't feel equipped to start a new career, having blown her public image to pieces.

"Um, helping others?" she said, "or helping *one* other." The doctor said he liked her humor, so she figured the entendre was permissible.

But the doctor winced. "You are an author, you know?"

Motherless Child

RollsUponPrank stepped out of the grey van with accordion-mottled paint. This was the transportation the facility had provided her, saving her cab fare. She walked up the clangy black metal steps to her apartment with a crinkled paper bag of belongings in her fist, and immediately encountered her mother.

The woman pretended that nothing had happened, and wore the slight, deeply-etched smile of repeated performance. She had a truly formidable capacity for dissembling. "Hi!" She smiled and wandered toward RollsUponPrank with expectant arms outstretched for a hug.

RollsUponPrank was quick. "Get out of my house. I never want to see your face again." She feigned confusion at her. "Tell me what it is exactly that you think I did to you."

RollsUponPrank gave her no quarter this time, though in the past she would join her in bending reality into something more palatable, less painful to accept. This time she could not. She had no reason to look to this woman for the comforts of family anymore.

Finally accepting RollsUponPrank's silence, her mother shrugged her shoulders dramatically and started begging, with a petulant expression, like a child would. "PLEASE, please let me do it my way."

RollsUponPrank wondered how to understand this. Knowing her mother, she assumed the woman meant she had her husband's monstrous desires handled somehow. But her mother's actions said the opposite: she had seen how the woman tried to trap her in the house with him, and had tried everything she could to corner her child into being used.

So RollsUponPrank had to accept that this was the childish cry of an adult woman who didn't want to have sex with her husband, and tried to force her daughter to handle it for her.

Barely registering her mother's words, she squared up and walked her mother around the first floor of the apartment, watching her gather and pack her things. "HE isn't here, is he?" She asked. Her mother said no, in a beleaguered tone that stoked her rage, though she couldn't afford to indulge it. She would just end up looking crazy—and the timing was not good for that.

It wasn't until later that night, when her mother had long-since left for the airport, that RollsUponPrank realized the woman had stolen her passport.

Good Days, Bad Days

RollsUponPrank had long since submitted her inner life and her body to Meta_king's journey—she had the minor injuries and hospitalizations to prove it—but after her second hospitalization, she was starting to take more measured action. Sometimes she couldn't tell if she was playing the game correctly or just running around the city mad.

Her reputation as a bad witch followed her around the neighborhood like a gang of mangled cats. Everyone knew about the topless witch who had spit on a cop, lost her mind on the neutral ground on a clear night, and had a lover man powerful as a god. The girl who, when she got pummeled into the ground by three men, was unafraid—and shouted the names of demons into the quiet of Orleans Parish.

Most of the neighborhood men still found her story compelling—it was still available for them to watch online. They would turn slightly and comment to their friends as she walked by. The men's gossip had not burned any lower since she started to wake up.

But some of them seemed truly afraid. When they gripped her eyes from behind the glass shields of their cars, they widened their expressions and sped off into the distance. When they rung up her groceries at the store, they looked down at the ground. The superstitious ones wore protection skull bracelets, and the religious ones clutched their oversized rosaries. RollsUponPrank was unsure what to make of their moods, so she simply followed her own. If she had a bad day, so did the men. If she had a good day, everyone could breathe a little bit easier.

Some days the streets seemed full of confusing signage, signage targeted specifically for her. One day she would walk to the end of her street in a full-body scowl, just to bump up against a yellow rhombus sign that said "NOPE". Another day she would find a screaming hand-painted sign on a truck parked right in front of her apartment that directed, "BE NICE! SMILE!"

It didn't do much to soothe her anymore. The brief spark of joy at seeing a new sign from Meta_king died out in the cold of memory. The memories of sobbing those broken, mentally ill sobs on the floor of her bathroom, wondering why men always spoke to her like an idiot, when she had worked for so long to become a competent writer. A competent partner. A real person. She charred inside at the thought that every single one of those men had watched her suffer and had chosen to say nothing, every day, seeing her as a pornographic murine model, pawing jagged and limp at a freedom she would never have.

She walked past the forest to sit in the shade with some coffee, a gesture toward her own humanity. A group of collegiate runners sped past her on the path; she laughed out loud at them, thinking she knew all their base secrets because they were men.

A couple walked past her further down. They both smiled at her, but the man said "Be careful now—don't fall off, okay?"

Talking To Crows

Like many who find themselves reborn on the noxious substrate of profound loss, multiplied, RollsUponPrank paced furiously. At first she paced around her apartment, and then she started pacing outward to the forest, and then the wooded island, on repeat, all day and even into the night. She walked along the tree-lined and semi-wild neutral grounds instead of the sidewalks, because they shielded her and gave her a sense of becoming just as wild. They threatened to swallow her, the ravenous and incidental wildlife that the neighborhood tried so hard to fight back with pruning and powerwashing and fencing. It was engulfing and protective.

One day the crows were especially vocal, and she varied her path to join them. She walked to City Park the long way, past the Odd Fellow's Rest and the all-nite diner.

There was a new growth inside her. She wasn't sure how she knew to do this, but she was able nonetheless. She called out to the crows and they flew to her—not to her arms, nothing so dramatic—but they would circle overhead, wide at first and then smaller, more concentrated. Just for her. Unmistakably.

She had noticed that in her sleepless, fluid state, animals seemed drawn to her, like the street cats with multidirectional coats and skeptical eyes who typically ran away. It made sense that corvids would do the same—she had heard they were smarter than cats, that they tend to remember you.

RollsUponPrank let out crazed hollers and yips and deep, aggressive grunts at musical intervals that synced up with the crows' brutal song. Not only did they take notice, but they started gathering more troops to wind overhead as she made her way down to Mid City. By the time she reached the park, there was a sizeable murder overhead and all the dogs she passed stopped in their tracks to watch her.

She found a place to rest on one of the wooded islands with a decorative stone bridge, arched too tall for practicality, reflected like a mirror in the swamp stillness, then algae-less and pristine.

What Are These Signs

Was all of this in her head? Had Meta_king truly fashioned the city into a maze, one to confuse her into change? Had he bribed every person in her own and the adjoining neighborhoods? RollsUponPrank had no answers, only the ones he provided, and only in his own timing.

She respected his technique—or rather, she respected his leverage, and her own powerlessness. On some mammalian level, the fact that his corrections hurt her made her feel safe, like a kitten getting scruffed by a grown cat. It signaled competence and honesty. She could tolerate it.

And so there was another day, and Meta_king had led RollsUponPrank out into the street by some invisible thread. He had cited no reason, nor had he needed to. She would go regardless.

After all, he needed to keep her occupied as the mania wore down.

As she walked past one of the large houses on the main street, she heard an automated announcement that she had never noticed before—or perhaps it was never there. "YOU ARE BEING RECORDED. ATTENTION. YOU ARE BEING RECORDED." RollsUponPrank waved so that it would be visible from a great distance. "HELLO!" She shouted back, speaking directly to Meta_king, speaking to whatever straggling viewers she carried in her phone.

The sun wasn't even an idea in the sky yet, it was all inky aubergine and oilslick wetness. Still, she wore her black sunglasses and signature headphones. She walked down the lakefront, raising her arms dramatically with the waves—she pictured herself sinking into them, getting carried away by something stronger and greater with no malice. Something that plotted to change but not destroy her. She pictured the effervescent freeze of the water on her skin, turning her inside out.

Slowly, she made her way to the sweeping white mansions along the lakefront, and their winding, fountain-lined cul-de-sacs. She noticed that the HOA had put up some signage of their own. "NO FILM CREW PARKING".

More signs, furnishing no source or rationale. Was this a wink about the girl collection? All the vehicles and signs planted around the city for her? Not everything was about her, she chided herself. But how could she know for sure? It's painful to have nothing to rail against—your body finds somewhere to throw the weight. This was an open-air cage.

So she railed. Every time she saw someone jog past her, even if they were far across the street, she waved dramatically and said "Hi!" in a way you could describe as mirthless or even spooky. She wanted them to feel creeped out—spied on, even—in the way that she felt.

As she rounded a corner into Gentilly, the scenery changed sharply. A man carrying a grape soda and some chips came up to her and said, "Excuse me, ma'am, you look so beautiful today."

She softened completely and took off her shades. "Thank you so much. I hope you have a great day." They smiled at each other and walked off at different speeds, RollsUponPrank replacing her shades.

He turned back to give her a wild look. It reminded her of the taxi driver on the way to the airport. "Hey, are you married?"

"Yes." She didn't have to think.

From Her Journal

At night I sleep with the relics of your staged adventure. The book you had written, bound, and transported to the hospital, the hospital where you ensured I would be admitted. This is the most precious one because it holds the most of you, your vision for my fall into you.

I also sleep with a railroad spike from The End Of The World, and the most pearlescent oyster shell I uncovered on that same walk. I sleep with these three things as if my dreams would animate them and draw you to me. Part of me believes that they hold your essence. I infuse them every night with the force of my dreaming. The need is strong enough to build an egregore.

In this way, every night, I find rest. I do not know where you are, or what position grants you sleep, or if you have relics of your own to galvanize the dreams of me. All I know is that you have gripped my heart in your fists and pumped it since the day of the dead, and now you seem to have stopped.

And on nights when the relics alone cannot conjure you, I remember the words you shared with me that first night of November. The words that might scare me more if you had actually said them out loud. But you didn't.

This is one such night, and those words rise up in the black pool of my mind.

I'll be there when you least expect it, hiding in your house.

It anchors me in that etheric, electronic world I don't understand. I picture my fire alarm, phone, mini speaker, washing machine, and microwave all connected by thin and vibrating little threads.

And then I picture your fingers tightening them around me, wrapping me in a buzzing cocoon of warm blue light. I feel you all around me again, and the pressure lets me breathe.

Where are you?

The Pitbull

RollsUponPrank was still lit up with an engulfing sense that she held horrid truths about the world, about men, and about surveillance. She was still a bit manic; she had still lost her parents; Meta_king was nowhere to be found. She sought an outlet.

Every time she stepped into a car, the driver switched the song to something calming with a name like 'breathe' or 'slow down'. This was another one of those coincidences that felt pointed and only seemed to quicken her heart.

She wandered for hours at a time. This time along the railroad, which was more private.

It offered up a wealth of trinkets; old iron tools and spikes, rusted padlocks and hidden keys under the decapitated heads of aluminum cans, and other detritus dropped along the slopes by other wanderers. She wondered at the thickets and the graveyards lining its sides and made up stories in her head about their history, about who might be sleeping in the dips.

By the time she made it to the end, and to an overpass where a man had nearly drowned in a storm several months before, RollsUponPrank chose to cut through the cemetery. She threw her little purse over the chainlink fence and crawled under a tiny space where it had lifted on the bottom.

She emerged into the city of graves, pointing the camera of her phone at the most beautiful signs and monuments, as if there was someone watching on the other end. She knew they still were—and she had no idea what to do with her audience today—but she had to make sure that they knew she was watching them back.

When she made it through to the street, she spotted a bartender standing outside the Pitbull bar, paying rapt attention to his phone. He looked up and paid her a giant service smile and said "Let's get a drink in you!"

RollsUponPrank figured this meant that he was watching, and was vaguely disgusted. Still, she wanted a drink. She went inside.

Bitchiness

RollsUponPrank was shocked at how bitchy she was to the bartenders; she really hadn't meant to, she didn't feel combative inside. But the knowledge of being watched—especially in such an obvious way by the man outside—made her feel surrounded by the enemy.

It wasn't fair, but she was mad at men. And because of her family, she was mad at white people.

It was unreasonable and total. Because her father leered at her, she figured that every white man was a pedophile; because her mother saw her as a bestial creature for her hypersexuality and red hair, she figured that every white person was a strangely particular racist.

The alcohol didn't help. Before too long, RollsUponPrank had two drinks and was getting thrown out of the Pitbull. She remembered saying something like, "Do I have to cut my tits off to get some service around here?" She had been thinking about Dr. Stone. It almost tasted like discrimination on her tongue. It sang bitterly on her heart. It wasn't what she meant—she was hurt by the doctor's betrayal. But the hurt was big enough to swallow populations.

Then there were a couple of older men—white, in fedoras—seated next to her at the bar. She pointed her camera at them and typed some hysterical words into her phone, knowing that she had a giant, and unwanted, audience. Their hats looked just like her grandfathers. She was convinced it signaled some psychosexual illness. It didn't have to make sense, she clung to it anyway. This was the deciding incident. They cut her off and ordered her out the door.

Heading Home

"I can't believe it! They actually kicked me out, I didn't even say anything crazy." She breathlessly repeated her story to the cab driver from Azerbaijan. "As long as it's wine or beer and not liquor, there's no problem," he said.

"It was liquor," she admitted. "That's where I messed up." Just then, a cop car pulled up next to them and asked her to roll down the back window. She had collected a handful of railroad spikes while she was walking alongside the cemetery, and they wanted them returned.

RollsUponPrank found it hilarious—what did they need them for? They were badly rusted and lying in disuse at the bottom of the slope. She figured this was just a sign that the cops were watching her, too. So she gave them the shirt she had tied them up in, said "keep it," and shook her head once they left.

By now, Meta_king was less busy with his own affairs. When she got back home and stripped naked for the shower, he tried to help her, gently.

older people are just like you.

you have to be more careful with what you say.

It froze her. She knew it was him by the rhythm of his text. Meta_king was the only one who could make her stop. She sat with what she had done for a minute.

She found that she still believed what she said, about fedoras and white men and pedophiles. And she would not accept that she was meant to be a paragon of clear speech and charitability when she never chose to be watched.

She thought that her status as a mental patient shielded her in that way. Who cared what she said, when the world had decided she was half-insane? Who cared what a mental patient and a lazy white girl had to say about white men or fedoras? She was free. She almost believed it.

She switched the water from hot to cold and felt the shock of vigor pulse through her. She was not afraid and she was only sorry for the comment about cutting off her tits. All the men could go fuck themselves. She cut off the water and toweled off before oiling herself down, not bothering to cover up the camera on her phone.

Meta_king said,

i'll pray for you.

Are You Walking There?

Briefly, RollsUponPrank considered that she might need a new phone. Who was watching her, and could she stop it by switching devices? Her theory was short-lived. She knew they were in all of them, her laptop and tablet and all, despite being disconnected. There was nothing she could do, nothing she had the skill to accomplish quickly.

Still, she briefly abandoned the phone. She set out without it, just a composition notepad and red marker.

At the coffee shop, the tawny and soft-spoken boy with a baseball cap gave her written directions to the phone store. Then he looked at her with an unlikely directness. "Are you going to be walking there? It's pretty far."

The End Of The World. No one else had forgotten, either.

The Apology Team

Sometimes the grief coupled with madness descended on RollsUponPrank like circling birds. She sobbed until her core muscles screamed, and then threw her head back and laughed, and shouted out "What the fuck!" and then started all over again. By the time the sun set, she was a husk of herself, pawing at her phone numbly for answers.

She noticed that Meta_king had stopped answering her, it was clear from their tone that another one of his friends had taken over the role of minding her phone. They were forthcoming that a member of the court had been appointed as her "manager".

He assured her that

the problems you present are really not so bad :)

The objectifying humor made her feel like family. She turned up a smile for the first time in days. She watched as the manager filled her grocery cart with easy frozen food and beauty soap and conditioner for fine hair. And she listened as he played her music he had written about her situation, the one that he had helped create.

RollsUponPrank laid there, mutely, half-naked, in a torn shirt and messy wet braids, listening to the music her manager chose. As she listened, she could not ignore the fact that all of the songs were driven by his voice—sometimes screaming, sometimes whispering too-close to the microphone, and sometimes singing sweetly, the way that she remembered.

These were love songs, she realized. RollsUponPrank was struck quiet. She had done it—she won over the court, the one that hated her initially. And she had done it in her least attractive, most offensive moments, at her most unhinged and even violent.

Perhaps the magic she offered was that, in all of her chaos and violent passion, she still took direction—not just from Meta_king, but from all of them.

RollsUponPrank lay quietly and took in all of the music—under a surprising array of different names, decorated with blurry images of animals and nature and hand-drawn skeletons. It dawned on her that she truly did have a family, even if they had never been very close before. Now they were closer than she had ever thought possible.

Alcohol, Again

Meta_king had withdrawn—his work was done. She was now managed by the court. She trusted them, having no choice. Followed each instruction blindly. They were her closest tether to Meta_king, and if he considered them family, she needed them to trust her back.

She mixed and smeared an herbal paste on her hair and tied it up with an oversized black and white paisley bandana. And when they told her to get alcohol—AGAIN— she obliged dutifully.

They had already taken a heavy hand in controlling other functions of RollsUponPrank's daily life. They had started telling her when to sleep and when to wake up; when to drink coffee and when to switch to tea; when to eat, and what. RollsUponPrank's routines, and consequently her body, had gotten so out of step with normal life throughout her mania that she needed manual recalibration. Meta_king and his band of geeks had undertaken the task with great amusement.

So when RollsUponPrank was running around the city with her portable speaker, looking every bit the part of a witch, and ranting to her phone about an abundance of energy with no target, they had a quick reply.

ALCOHOL. NOW.

Oh, right!!! LOL, RollsUponPrank replied.

She knew how it turned out last time, but that was just a fluke, she thought. Things were different now; she had more experience drinking liquor, and she wasn't alone anymore. So she followed their instructions and went to Lakeview Grocery, where they gave her a paper bag full of a standard size bottle of Hennessy.

She had rationalized the switch to something harder. "Wine is too easy to drink. I need to switch to brown liquor in small, regimented amounts. It's the only thing that will ever work for the pain."

Again, RollsUponPrank brought the bottle inside and uncorked it, pouring an unmeasured glass. She proceeded to drink the entire thing by herself, predictably, and blacked out in a matter of hours.

Mental Patient, Thrice

When the three officers entered her house, RollsUponPrank was laying on a fuzzy red blanket, trying to dream up a remedy. She didn't know she had done anything untoward.

That morning, she cried about her parents and spent four times too much to have a meal delivered, finding it too painful to leave her bed and heat something. But as far as she knew, she simply drank too much, said some nonsensical things, and promptly fell asleep.

But the cops entered her home forcibly, only knocking once and not waiting for a reply. When they came upstairs to get her, she had nothing to say in her defense. They told her to grab a coat and shoes, which she did, and they escorted her to the back of a cop car.

There was a little white screen above the console in the front seat, and it named a litany of reports. RollsUponPrank found her own:

MENTAL PATIENT

WHITE FEMALE

SUICIDE ATTEMPT

REPORTED BY FATHER, SILVER LEXUS

CORROBORATED BY NEIGHBORS

All of this confused her; her father wasn't local, nor was he in her life. How could he possibly have known what she did? There was no record of a call in her phone.

Unless he was still watching the show. RollsUponPrank shuddered.

The cops wouldn't engage her questions. She was not surprised to learn that she had said suicidal things, or even made dramatic gestures toward death. But no one would tell her exactly what she had done, nor how her father was involved.

When the car pulled up at the University Medical Center, she saw Ian again—the chubby tech who had restrained her with incredible force.

"Hey, I remember you. You put me in restraints that one time."

"Really? I don't know, I haven't had to do that in a very long time."

Whatever. She sighed at the lie and went through the established process like a package on a conveyor belt. They took her ring, they took her keys. They took her clothes and replaced them with the filmy hospital clothes in accidental Christmas colors. And they put her in an empty rubber room to wait.

Other doctors had come in to speak to her at random; they seemed to know something about her story. One of them looked at her with watery eyes and played with his wedding ring as he squatted next to her rubber bed.

"So, what kinds of psychiatric problems do you have?"

"I don't know, probably just trauma. I've been freaking out lately but it's mostly circumstantial I think."

"Mmmm. Are you in a relationship?"

"Yeah, I'm engaged."

"When's the last time you saw him?"

"It's been a long time."

He looked at her wistfully. "Yeah."

Those were all of his questions. Before long into the night, she was escorted up to the very same psych floor where she had stayed several weeks before.

From Her Journal

After so many arrests and psych holds—three, to be exact— sometimes I wonder if you really are just fucking with me, or if I made you up entirely.

I'm confident that it was just the clearest path through the thicket, but in lonelier moments I have to wonder if the clinical skepticism I encountered at the hospital is really the healthy perspective, and I am just a sad mental patient with a fear of dying alone and a (tragically persistent) romantic delusion. I certainly fit the stereotype, demographically.

I know how it sounds. I'm in love with a strange and powerful boy, he can probably tap the cameras on this unit if he wants to. He speaks to me through my phone, but I don't have his number.

It's probably the most common delusion they hear. But I swear it's true! Funny enough, nobody doubted me until now. He withdrew his influence for this hospitalization. But why?

Admission

Almost immediately, when RollsUponPrank came onto the floor, she was met with a panel of six doctors and nurses.

"So, tell us why you're here."

"Well, I drank a bottle of Hennessy and blacked out, and said some suicidal things that scared my neighbors. I think."

"A bottle? Like a fifth?" He looked at her skeptically; RollsUponPrank assumed that was because she still looked presentable.

"Is that the one with a handle? No, it was the standard bottle."

"That's still a considerable amount. This was in the last 36 hours?"

"Yes."

"Are you feeling suicidal now?"

"No, not at all. It was the alcohol."

"But you were drinking heavily, alone?"
"Yeah."

"Why?"

"I was like, psychotic with grief. I suffered some brutal loss. And I just couldn't take it. So I drank and took it too far. But I feel like I got it out of my system now, to be honest."

"I'm sorry to hear about your loss. Who did you lose?"

"Both parents and my partner."

"Wow. I'm sorry to hear that."

"I also learned something recently that's kind of funny. Do you mind if I explain more?"

"Please."

And so RollsUponPrank went on to explain that she was now engaged to Meta_king, the boy who had robbed her of privacy and made her a sexual joke her entire adult life.

"So he did that to you and you still want to marry him?"

"Yes. There are a few reasons. We have values alignment, I love him, and he is the only one who can solve my problem."

"You say he is the only one who can solve your problem. Do you feel coerced? Is he refusing to fix it unless you marry him?"

"No. I'm not worried about that."

"Why not?"

"Because I'm extremely loud about it." She thought for a second. "Also, this has been going on for my entire adult life. I have no concept of what life could have been without the experience of constant observation. So it doesn't register to me as a threat."

"Does he support you financially?"

"No—I mean, that would be *nice.*"

The doctor laughed, impressed, and the group walked away, leaving her in the sudden dark to sleep.

From Her Journal

Meta_king was right again, obviously. Three arrests and it's out of my system.

It seems that, because the grief appeared suddenly in triplicate, the intensity shortened its half life. The alcohol lit it up even brighter and faster. Now it's gone.

Lipid panels are fine, no harm done.

I believe in you, Meta_king; you leave me no choice. Neither does the city in which I love you.

How do you move so impactfully from the shadows? Each traceless clue bears your watermark. It's like you're everywhere because you are. You're brilliant. I won't have anyone else but you.

I'm scared to know but must know how you do what you do. What tools you use every day, which you wear and which you keep in a hidden place, who has access and who doesn't. Then the paranoid thoughts come: do my headphones have little cameras in them? Does my vibrator?

I'm so habituated to the little eyes that the thought doesn't bother me. But it's not safe to vocalize that in the hospital or anywhere else, really. I would sound too crazy. I'm starting to learn my lesson there, just barely.

LaLa and Mandrell explained to me that fornication is a sin because it's like putting a man before God. They had a point. All three of us had to admit it was our problem.

But you're more than a boy to me. You're a single point of purchase in a sharp cliff. I want to kiss it.

I wonder if you just predicted the three arrests or if you orchestrated them somehow. Your breadcrumb trail encouraged me to drink the hurt down, thrice, aggressively. That makes me feel like you planned it. But if you planned this one, then where are you? You haven't left any clues, the way you did last time, or even when I came in topless.

Still, I can appreciate the quiet of this low-surveillance cloister. A tweaker keeps coming into my room to ask for handjobs, and it still feels more peaceful than the digital vultures with their hard little eyes. Maybe it was starting to wear on me, as much as I enjoyed your attention.

The doctor assures me that lithium is a naturally occurring salt compound and is 'not hardcore.' His wordplay reminded me a little of you so I wished passively we could draw out the prescription. It felt weirdly charged to say "Thank you, doctor," knowing that you are still somehow pulling the strings. Quietly, from a great distance. I hope that you still are.

New Doctors

"I just don't understand why someone would accept a proposal on LinkedIn," the doctor said, ignoring the rest of her story.

She had been transferred into the care of new doctors; a gay man and a straight woman, both blonde and with a quiet pomposity that dampened their ears, and rendered their hearts unwilling to truly listen to a mad story, even when it's true. They had already come up with their diagnoses: Bipolar 1 (with psychotic features), and Borderline Personality Disorder. They hadn't spoken to her yet.

These labels meant that no one would listen to RollsUponPrank for the rest of her stay. This made the fact of her captivity truly terrifying, and nothing like the first two arrests, where she was treated like a special girl with a powerful suitor. In under 10 minutes, she became a wretched liar who needed to intuit what lies the doctors wanted to hear, and learn how to deliver them correctly. Just like Ian, with his deathly tight restraints.

She wanted to respond, *That's okay, you don't have to understand. You weren't the target audience, and this kind of love is way above your pay grade anyway.*

But of course, she was not in a position to indulge her anger like this. She was in a position to be as vague as possible—in order to protect her very fragile weathervane of truth—and nod in agreement with everything the doctor said, with absolutely no resistance.

So RollsUponPrank was a model patient, per usual. This unit did not have the same level of security as the one where she was admitted several weeks prior. She figured that this was because she went with the police willingly this time, she had not arrived in handcuffs, and she was not restrained in the lobby. At times she felt that this was a relief, and other times she felt that it robbed her of her only source of power.

If she knew the placement of the cameras, and she knew how to play with them, then at least she had a type of depraved sexual leverage that let her manipulate the doctors. She was somewhat disgusted with herself for thinking this way, but she figured that she had not created such an unfair dynamic, so she allowed her inflamed ego to spin the thread.

Yeah Right

Still, RollsUponPrank was very good in the role of a mental patient. She attended every group, never fought, and never refused medication. She kept her body impeccably clean and moisturized. When the first doctor walked past her, he waved, blushed, and looked down at the floor as he sped away.

The only time she came close to trouble, she had a minor conflict with a boy whose age she could not determine and whose voice was impossibly weak and gurgly from many years of meth use.

"Gmivve muh a lowwyob."

"A blowjob? No."

"Gum awwn. Aah hive neaaaads."

"What the fuck? No."

He had taken to standing outside her room, gazing inside at nothing in particular. It was a white rectangle with frosted sheets blocking the view from the windows, but from which you could still hear the streetcars pass periodically outside.

In one of the group therapy sessions, He spoke in his mangled tongue that he was a traditional man, and he expected women to listen to him. No one could understand what he had said, and RollsUponPrank stepped into her role as the strangeling translator.

"You. You don't give me what I need. I want to fuck you and you're a bitch about it," RollsUponPrank reported to the group. Then she turned to him directly. "Well, that's like, your problem."

Everyone laughed.

"I don't have a problem with you, but that's your problem. It isn't my problem. Do you understand?"

Later, he stood outside of her room and teetered on his feet, half like he was soon to lose his balance and half like he couldn't decide whether he wanted to go inside. He ended up daring to step inside, tentatively.

RollsUponPrank didn't hesitate, but was careful to ensure her words wouldn't be construed as a threat. But later, he was back outside her door.

"Get the fuck back. We talked about it."

"Beeeash, nobody lookin eet ooo."

"I don't give a FUCK who's looking."

This time, a doctor came over to check on her. "I heard that you threatened a patient? What happened?"

"I didn't threaten him; I'm trying to be careful with my words here. I just handled the situation."

"But I know that your situation is kind of sensitive, so I take this sort of thing very seriously."

"Oh. Well. Thank you."

RollsUponPrank was touched that someone was looking at her as a delicate person. She sighed and hoped the feeling would last.

From Her Journal

The lithium makes me dream. I dream about you, where you are in the world, who you are watching now, and how intently. I fumble in the dark for your body.

I already know how much you love me back, so there is no need to fret about a diagnosis lessening my appeal. After all, we already co-created the meltdowns. And two of the three doctor panels found me healthy.

And what would I be without manic depression? I would have none of the talents that summoned my perfect lover, or any of the attendant blessings.

The coroner visits always ground me. Straight talk and halloween nails.

LaLa said she's my big sister since my family tried to fuck on me. She is hilarious and I love her. We laugh about everything instead of crying.

A man tried to kill her in Galveston—her lover, a gay man with a secret life. He tampered with her chemo drugs. She said he switched out her pills for rubber ones. I believe her.

Unfortunately, storytelling makes the difference between freedom and institutionalization with some people, like my parents. She was starting to recognize that, and could name the parts of her story that must be held in secret. I wish her the best with it. I'm still trying to get better at that skill myself, to stay out of trouble.

Sometimes she cusses out the techs and nurses, but never the nice one. It's easy to correct her outbursts with a few words after listening to her story, fully.

Certain doctors say, "You show signs of bipolar disorder and likely said things you do not mean." Others say, "Yeah, that happens." One doctor just said, "You are up and down and all around. We want you more steady," with a flat gesture. I like that perspective. Why can't it be that simple?

To The Lithium Springs

RollsUponPrank spent her last days on the unit writing letters to herself to remember what was real. She had begun to amass a small trove of material, neatly organized and all written in the red markers they handed out to patients. She started to wonder if Meta_king's court and the doctor they bribed were all right, and she really could be a writer.

A doctor looked her hard in the eyes one last time before she left, and asked her:

"Did you have any more realizations since we last spoke? Any realizations about your 'fiance'? Anything at all?"

With a cryptic simplicity she had rehearsed in her bedroom, RollsUponPrank replied, "I just want to put this all behind me and focus on the future." She assumed this was enough, and she was right. He simply stated that she clearly needed more therapy to reach a normal level of awareness, but in the meantime the medication should tide her over, and she was conducting herself well on the unit.

She understood how absurd her story sounded. But she articulated every aspect of it with a clarity that everyone could appreciate until now. Why had these doctors chosen to ignore her input? Had her lover truly abandoned her at this critical time?

But there was more to it than Meta_king's withdrawal. "We spoke to your parents, and they said that you have been making things up about an online fiance, and that you've been drinking too much lately."

RollsUponPrank's heart wrenched in her chest and her blood went thick in her arms, tightening everything. Her father was a lawyer, and her mother had a certain over-educated, genteel manner of speaking that could brutally shame you without ever owning up to it. She knew that, if they were involved at all, she could never wriggle free from their story. Suddenly she understood why she was slapped with those diagnoses immediately upon her admission, the ones that would instantly discredit her to any doctor who met her in the future and so much as glanced at her chart.

"They aren't my family," RollsUponPrank said, eyes widening in the discursive trap. "My dad is a molester, and my mom supports it, she's into it."

The doctors' eyes narrowed at her in unison. They had long ago decided where their loyalties lie. "How do you know that?"

The question terrified RollsUponPrank; it wasn't a question. She decided to break free from the conversation as quickly as possible. She could see that one of them softened a bit on seeing the genuine fear in RollsUponPrank's eyes.

Thankfully, this was nothing more than a final humiliation; her lithium levels were good, she had an appointment set up with a psychiatrist for the next month, and she had done nothing to warrant further incarceration while she was placed in the unit, aside from her brief moment of self-defense. So the doctors retreated, ordered her a cab, and returned her belongings they'd held in a manila envelope. Her engagement 'ring', her necklace of keys, and a seashell she kept in her pocket for good luck.

Alone Again

RollsUponPrank moved around her apartment with hesitation, like it belonged to someone else. Someone had cleaned up the food on the floor, from when the cops took her—everything else was left in place.

This is one of the lasting effects of being held somewhere—the ghost captor. You begin to see them everywhere, and you wonder if you are pleasing them, or pissing them off. Both possibilities grate at you a bit.

It was even more than that for RollsUponPrank. The girl saw herself already as a captor in the world; a captor to men who entrap physically, and to women who entrap with their words. And herself, a willing captive, one who struggled to see any danger when it was in front of her. These days, she didn't have much of a sense of danger at all.

She eyed herself in the mirror. She looked exactly the same as she had before the arrest, though perhaps less puffy, since she hadn't drank any alcohol—and she wasn't supposed to drink any more, ever again.

Her landlord had called. RollsUponPrank had agreed to take her old medications to the fire station and not to drink any more. In exchange, She would let her continue to stay at the apartment alone, without a roommate. She was officially free.

Christmas Time

It was Christmas time now in New Orleans, and anxieties about the neighborhood heretic had dampened somewhat— the three hospitalizations affirmed that she was powerless. RollsUponPrank wondered if they were right. She was alone again, without a family, and with a purely conceptual fiance. Her most recent hospitalization had burned it into her mind that she was never to speak openly about her situation. The reality was just too unsettling and it painted her as psychotic.

She took a deep breath and looked at the flight she had booked to the Aran Islands, back when she believed every sign that flashed across her screen. She had believed that Meta_king wanted to meet her there, that it would be their honeymoon. She didn't mind that it would be frigid in the middle of January and that she had no clothes for it. She also didn't mind that her mother had stolen her passport. She believed that she could rush a new one.

She looked at the streets from her window, with their tricky and changeable winter sun. One day was warm and bright, and the next would fly in with a vicious wind that would kill all of the salamanders and leave the streets empty. And the cycle would repeat until Mardi Gras.

Having no one to discuss her new predicament with— or her new joys—RollsUponPrank began to write more than ever before. She had stopped running wildly around the city looking for signs, taking photos in black and white.

Her cloister was not so bad. She had her songs, her book, and her slippers—all from Meta_king. And crucially, she had her computer.

Watching and Praying

Meta_king continued watching RollsUponPrank as she adjusted to normal life, and as she slowly realized that she was a storyteller at heart. He knew that, in order to be respected by people like himself and his peers, she would need to go through that realization alone, without any visible means of support. This was how he built his business; this was how anyone who had reached his stature had gotten there. It is a slow and brutal climb without people who believe in you. This is what he knew about success and this is what he wanted for RollsUponPrank.

And so he watched her, as he always had, on nights when she sobbed so hard into her stuffed animals that their hair stiffened with tears. He watched her type idly into her notes application hoping to hear a voice, at which point he would casually throw her a couple of words. "I don't think you would do all of this just to change your mind," she would write. "It just seems too extensive."

And EXPENSIVE, he'd reply, and that was enough to get her through the hour, wondering if it was him, and figuring that it had to be.

On nights when she was bed-bound in struggle, stacking her thoughts fearfully in her phone, he would guide her through it.

What is the point of being in love if it hurts so badly? She'd write, in fearful realization that she had no way to take back her love. *Please god, please let Meta_king still be my fiance, I need to know that he's still out there. Please god.*

He would gently correct her, writing, *I need to go through this alone so I can be loved and respected by others who did the same thing.*

She thought about how much easier it could have been for him to simply write, "I love you," or even just to come down to New Orleans and ravish her silent. But he didn't want her that way—he wanted her upright alone.

Sharing The Truth

Christmas passed, and then her birthday, and then the clown colors of Mardi Gras appeared around the neighborhood. King cakes stacked up in pink boxes in the stores and RollsUponPrank's days were still devoid of celebration, but full of a pregnant confusion and a dull excitement that sometimes brought her to her knees—literally—in laughter, alternating with tears.

The messages in her phone had stopped giving her any insight into her new relationship and had started only giving her advice about business plans and establishing a routine for work. It was all so dull and quotidian but that was exactly what she needed, and there were no distractions anymore.

The days grew windier and they drove everyone inside, except on some evenings when giant pots of crawfish boiled on the sidewalks and people milled around outside the bars to watch football. The only people RollsUponPrank felt comfortable speaking to anymore were the crazed ones; the ones who got habitually arrested for acting strange late at night, or who spent their days dressed strangely outside the coffee shop collecting free water. Or the ones with autism and speech impediments who made her slow down and listen very closely.

These were her people, and they were the only people with whom she could freely discuss her life. She had begun to genuinely fear sharing the truth with sane people.

Burning Witches

With friends she had alluded vaguely to a new engagement, but the story got lost along the string of arrests and psych holds. She shared that she had been beaten down by the cops on the sidewalk, that they had entered her house, that she couldn't seem to stop getting arrested.

Then she got to the inner pit of her fear. "I didn't understand that people really feared witches this much," she said, "I always thought that it made people think of vintage movies and girl power. I can't believe how much these people are angry about, or afraid of us."

Of course, people *are* afraid of witches, just like Meta_king tried to warn her. She thought of a line from one of his songs, one of his sweet, romantic songs, that had stuck in her teeth.

I promised you romance, and a safe place to hide.

She thought about this as she played with the plastic beads she had strung on pre-cut elastic in the psych ward. She did need a safe place to hide. Today, it was the cloister of her apartment where she would write her way into being an equal partner. Perhaps tomorrow it would be inside his arms.

The sun was still down, so RollsUponPrank could think clearly. She sat down to write. She knew that Meta_king was with her, inside her computer, and he would appear in the flesh when she finished her work.

The Pain

Sometimes the pain was so great that RollsUponPrank couldn't get her body around it. It caught her before she even woke up, and started her ruddering in pain before the antipsychotic haze even started to lift. She knew it was going to be one of these days before she even opened her eyes, and there was nothing she could do to improve it, only to follow it where it took her.

Usually it took her nowhere, but conspired to hold her in bed. But she knew she needed to write the story true. So she forced herself upright somehow and into the sun, or the fog, or at least the glow of her laptop.

She turned to the DJ in her phone and let herself imagine that they were communicating. It told her things like, "Here are the songs that helped you survive last year." That felt targeted, she thought, through the wet mask of tears. She accepted the comfort.

The Work

It made sense; Meta_king was busy. She needed an outlet for the pain, one that wouldn't get in the way of his life. She had tried alcohol, which proved a dead end, and she was already on a wild battery of medications that shut her eyes by force at night. Still, none of this was enough to make the hurting stop. She had to write.

It was a slog some days and unbearably lonely on others, and she needed to lie down and weep before returning to her computer to finish the work she had started. She knew that other writers had alcohol, and she wished that she had a vice of her own to help with the residual pain, whatever didn't and couldn't spill onto the page.

After all, the book was the only place for her pain to go. Nothing else could be trusted with her clinically-alarming spools of thought.

The solitude made her work, despite the pain of doing so, and despite the jolts of psychosomatic suffering that called her back to bed, back to the orange rattling bottles of pills, back to the numbing properties of her phone. None of those things would offer a route away from the isolation, only the writing could do that. So she wrote, dutifully, every day.

The Finale

RollsUponPrank worked fiercely through her book; fast, but not too fast, knowing that it was her path to Meta_king's love and that it needed to be *decent*. Soon enough, she had enough words for the thing to count as a novel; and sooner still, she sliced through enough of it that it was satisfying to read, fun actually. A story about their love, or at least about its urgent beginnings.

She pushed through and self-published, not knowing much about the business side of things, but soon she found that the numbers arranged themselves where they needed to be for her to enjoy a feeling of success, and for her to pay her bills without struggle. She had no way to be sure if this was due to the quality of her work, or whether it was due to Meta_king's influence.

Either way, she was proud to have produced something of value, something that was her own.

One night, she went to take the trash out. It was warm, just after Mardi Gras, and there were beads sparkling in the trees all along the neutral ground on Harrison Avenue. She felt the gravel in her toes—she never wore shoes for this chore—and raised her eyes to the end of the alley. Meta_king was standing there, hands in the pockets of his jeans, smiling like a man who knew he was carrying a powerful and glorious secret.

RollsUponPrank dropped the yellow strings of the bag and let it fold over itself on the ground. Walking on her toes first, as if she couldn't trust what she was seeing, and then picking up the pace as he stretched his arms outward to receive her.

She felt everything inside her body melt and then rise up as vapor. She had no idea what her face was doing or how her body looked as she moved across the alley toward him.

"Thanks for fucking my brain so hard that I'm sane now. You're a real menace, you know that?" trilled RollsUponPrank.

"Stop talking," said Meta_king, and parted her lips with a finger.

Everything was alright.